1

THE IMPRESSION OF JACK SULLIVAN

Sandy,
Hope you enjoy
this one!
Meredith

THE IMPRESSION OF JACK SULLIVAN

A Novel

Meredith Madden

ISBN 978-147-7562000

Text set in Times New Roman

Printed in the United States of America

First Edition 2012

ACKNOWLEDGEMENTS

Vonnegut wrote about the concept of a *karass*. It's brilliant. At some level, I'd like to think that this book speaks to that idea. I'm dedicating this book to the people who have mattered to my life in that way. Here is to each of you. Some of you will know who you are, others may not, and therein lies the beauty.

I am blessed amongst mothers. Ronan, I love you.

Thank you also to my parents, Peter and Linda Madden. They read the book in its earliest stages and championed it until the end. I love you.

I'm surrounded by great family. Thank you to my brothers, Peter and Nat, my sister-n-law, Jennifer, and my beautiful nieces, Rachel and Anna Madden. And in memory of my grandmother, who was truly one of a kind, Hazel Willmot.

Thank you to my early readers: Jennifer Hurley, Allison Kistner, Clem Madden, Colleen Madden, Susannah Jackson Park, and Colleen Ryan Soden. You are each amazing!

Thank you to Lorraine Berry and Leslie Daniels for always cheering me on and providing words of wisdom along the way.

It is important to me that I mention teachers who helped spark and sustain my love of learning and a passion for words, books, and writing. So, thank you to Ms. Maryann Pomroy Kowalsky, Mrs. Carolyn Buckley, Mr. Bob Evans, Mr. Jerry Pitarresi, Mrs. Helen Spector, Mr. Michael Klar, Mrs. Olga Mazzei, and Dr. Gretchen Lopez.

The Impression of Jack Sullivan

PLACES
Ithaca, New York 1962

There are places I have loved and places I have hated. Hyannis Port. I hated Hyannis Port. I hated Hyannis Port and I'd never even been to the damn place. Hyannis Port was never our annual summer vacation spot. We used to spend a week up north at a camp on Little Long Lake. We'd spent every July since I was five at that Adirondack camp. But all that changed over breakfast on the morning of my seventeenth year when Father said, "Hey, sport! How about a summer in Hyannis Port?"

Father's eyes twinkled. He closed the business section of the newspaper, straightened his tie, and gave me a sharp whack on the back, his sole display of paternal affection. He snatched his briefcase from the counter, shouted upstairs for my older brother, Thomas, to get his ass out of bed, then kissed Mother goodbye. He tossed an apple high in the air, caught it one handed, and sank his teeth down through the green skin with a crackling crunch. The white fruit bits sloshed around as he smacked his gums and nodded over at me, speaking while he chewed.

"Hyannis Port, Jack. You're going to love it," Father said.

I stared at Mother, drying dishes by the sink. The red gingham dish towel circled around the breakfast plate and my sight slipped into a checkered haze.

"Hyannis Port," I said aloud, just to make sure I was awake.

Mother bit her bottom lip and watched Father as he paraded down the driveway and bound into his spanking new 1962 powder blue Studebaker Lark. She reached her hand out toward the refrigerator door and slid her fingertips along a photo that she'd taken of Thomas and me romping around up north at the lake.

"Hyannis Port?" I said.

"It's where the Kennedys vacation," Mother said.

Ah, the Kennedys, I thought. For then it all made sense.

11

THE EARLY BIRD

I liked to wake up early. Liked to rise before the sun. Made me feel like I could really discover something if I woke up that early, especially while stuck in Hyannis Port at a lackluster Inn called The Honeysuckle. But all I wound up discovering were the half-empty tumblers scattered across the mahogany end tables and the colossal glass ashtrays brimming over with cigarette butts stained red from ladies' lipstick.

We'd arrived in Hynannisport yesterday afternoon. Father had gunned it down the sandy beach road. Hell, you would have thought there was a fortune waiting for him there. The place was hopping when we'd arrived. Lots of loud chatter filled the rooms. I didn't take a real good glimpse around. I was pretty wiped. I just waited in the foyer for Father to come back after signing us in and trudged up the mammoth staircase after him until I reached my room. I barely bothered to unpack a thing, favoring a good sleep after the long ride.

On the first morning I woke drowsy, but more interested in poking around the place and discovering what was in store for me over the month of July. I tip-toed through the main room, careful not to wake the poor soul passed out on the sofa, his wing-tipped shoes dangling over the edge. The main room smelt stale, like a loaf of frozen bread when it thaws. Smelt like something that should be fresh, but was having a hell of a hard time trying. What didn't smell stale was the scent drifting from the kitchen, so of course, that was where I headed.

On that Saturday morning, the Saturday morning after that party, the party that kicked off the summer of 1962 for the socialite families vacationing in Hyannis Port, Massachusetts, I found myself in the kitchen playing second fiddle to Ms. Maybelle Winson. Maybelle must have kicked off summer in her own way the night before because she was running around like a blind mouse not knowing where to go or what to do with itself.

She was tiny, Maybelle was. She was tiny in her bust, tinier still in her waist, why she was tiny straight on down to her feet which looked about the size of the feet on the elves at the Ithaca Firehouse Christmas parade last year. Ithaca, NY being my hometown. But never mind that, we were talking about Hyannis Port. Actually, we were talking about Maybelle. Maybelle and her munchkin feet, her pencil thin waist, her washboard chest and her…

"*Boy*! You've got ten minutes to brew that first pot of coffee, you hear? Ten minutes and that's all. Don't you stand there staring at me like you done wandered out of Mayberry now. Wake yourself up, boy, we've got work to do!" said Maybelle and her booming voice.

I fished my head through the hole of the apron that she'd flung at me. I found myself becoming the cat to her mouse, chasing her around the kitchen and saying things like, "Where's the coffee, ma'am? Where's the pot, ma'am? By the way, ma'am? I don't work here. I'm Jack Sullivan, ma'am. My family and I are guests at the Inn this July."

"Jack Sullivan, you say?" said Maybelle, stopping to turn and face me, tilting her head back and studying me like I was something she wasn't too sure of.

"Yes, ma'am," I said, offering my hand.

"Maybelle Winson," she said in a sugary sweet voice with a curtsy and a smile. The next thing I knew she thrust the coffee percolator straight into my gut and planted her mocha colored hand firm on my chest, driving me backward into the steel tub sink.

"Fill it all the way up with water. Coffee's already measured out in the bowl next to the stove. Put it on the burner and wait for it to come to a boil. You're down to five minutes. Now move!" she said. That Maybelle, she packed a punch.

As the percolator bubbled and the coffee brewed, I inhaled the bitter aroma floating in the air. My pride swelled like fingers in the heat. Victory, I thought. Triumph. I had made coffee, a whole pot. I *was* different than the flawed adolescents who slept late upstairs in the putrid named rooms of the Honeysuckle Inn. I hadn't woken, put on my tennis whites and gone flitting around the Hyannis Port tennis courts. No, of course I hadn't. I'd worked my morning away. My khaki shorts were covered with splotches of brown water and speckled with black grinds. I'd woken up early and *seized* my day. I…I…I was being yanked by my apron strings out onto the back porch.

"What do you think you're doing dragging me around like a rag doll?" I said.

"Oh, I'm sure you're somebody's doll, but you ain't mine," Maybelle said. "Now look down there at the end of the driveway, you see? Down where the silver mailbox is?"

"I see it," I said.

Maybelle straightened out my apron with two quick swipes of her hand. "Now, a truck's going to be pulling up there in ten minutes' time, green pickup. You'll hear it before you see it, clanks louder than a train engine. A man's going to pull over and his daughter's going to hop out with the Sunday papers, a whole stack of 'em. It's your job to take them from her and bring 'em back up to the Inn. If you're not there, they'll keep on driving. They keep on driving and my behind is out of a job. So you wait there until they show up. You understand me? Don't move a muscle until that truck stops and you get those papers from that girl. Then bring 'em back up here on the porch. If anyone sees you, say you were out on a walk and they just pulled over and you offered to help. Bring that stack and leave 'em right here by the back door. Open the screen door once and let it slam nice and loud, you hear? Then I'll know you got 'em alright. Leave your apron here with me, c'mon now take it off, take it off. No need for that anymore. Make sure you go back inside through the front door. Anyone catches you in the kitchen with me and I'll really hear it. Young white boy in the kitchen with me, Lord knows I'd never find a job anywhere on the Cape if that word got out. Now go on down there. Don't dawdle. I'd go myself but I've got to make the eggs. If breakfast's late again you won't be seeing my face 'round here no more. Though there's no reason why you should be seeing my face to begin with. Speaking of seeing my face, what'd you think you were doing sneaking into the kitchen this morning like that? My kitchen ain't no place for you, Mr. Jack Sullivan."

"Yes, ma'am," I said, standing stupefied at attention like a soldier in Maybelle Winson's personal army. With a swift turn of her heels, Maybelle went back inside. With a turn of mine, I was tripping down the porch steps and hustling toward the very spot where she'd told me to wait.

I looked at my watch. 6:34 a.m. I sat with my back against the white post holding up the mailbox. Just sat and listened. There's a lot that a good quiet morning can tell you. For one thing, the wind lapped soft against my left cheek so I figured the weather was going to be mild that day. It was a light, salty wind that brought to mind the saltwater taffy I'd stolen from my brother, Thomas's duffel bag the night before. The air smelled sweet like taffy, too, or maybe it was just those damn honeysuckles. The honeysuckles had to be around here somewhere, I thought, as I eyed the carved wooden sign on the sprawling lawn of the Inn.

I squinted up at the cloudless sky, and dug the heel of my sneaker into the dirt as dust flew out into the air. How did I get stuck at a place called the Honeysuckle Inn for the month of July? I wondered, shaking my head and biting down on my chapped bottom lip.

My best friend back home, Johnny Stewart, was spending his summer up in the Adirondacks, not far from the cabin where my family used to vacation. Johnny Stewart was at some camp where they hiked the High Peaks each week, built roaring bonfires, and slept on the bare earth beneath a canopy of stars.

Here I was trapped in a room named *Lily of the Valley*, sleeping underneath a canopy, an *actual* canopy, like the one in Johnny Stewart's sister's bedroom. Seventeen-years old and stuck peeking at a stash of nudie photos in a four poster bed under a white lace canopy; heck, I couldn't make any sense out of that.

All at once, I soared straight out of my skin, banging my head back against the wooden mailbox post. The noise was so loud that I thought the country was under attack. And wouldn't that be my luck, I thought, that I'd be stuck in Hyannis Port when the Cubans fired a missile at us. I looked up and saw that the sky was still crystal blue. If we were under attack, I was pretty certain I'd be seeing blazes by now. I jumped up and caught my breath, just in time to see a flash of green barreling straight at me.

I leapt back as the corroded pickup skidded to a stop at the tips of my sneakers. The blaring engine came to a lull as the man up front rammed the gear into park with a sharp whack of his hand. I took a deep breath, straightened my shirt, spit into my hand

and flattened the cowlick in my hair, then smiled. The passenger window rolled down and a hand reached over the top to lift up the handle from the outside. The door creaked opened, crying out for a splash of oil, and down jumped the girl that Maybelle had told me would deliver the newspapers.

"Papers," I said as my mouth gaped open. In my mind I could hear my mother telling me to close my mouth shut, and that it looked like I was catching flies. But as much as I tried, I just couldn't do it. As a matter of fact, I couldn't do much of anything.

"Here they are," she said, heaving them from out of the flatbed of the truck, the soles of her bare feet pressing into the earth, her creamy white calves lengthening as she reached for the pile.

"Papers," I said.

"That's all of 'em," she said, dropping the papers into my hands, then cocking her head to examine my face as she twirled her red hair, deep red as burgundy, like the wine I sipped each Sunday from the church chalice.

"Did Maybelle send you out here, son?" said the sturdy man from behind the wheel.

"Yes, sir," I said.

"Well then, she'll be expecting you, so you best get going on." He tugged on the rim of his cap. The girl hopped back into the passenger seat, reached around and pushed the handle down, then yanked the door shut.

"Yes, sir," I said as he shifted the gear into drive, shook the throttle, and sputtered on down the sandy beach road.

It was a clear Cape morning, but I walked in a fog back to the porch. The papers slid out from underneath my arm with a thud. I pulled open the screen door, a long, slow pull that screeched like an owl, then let it go with a bang against the white wooden frame. Inside, I could see Maybelle dancing her way from stove to sink to silver serving platter.

I stumbled down the porch steps and around to the front door. 7:07 a.m. Through the small door window the main room looked dark; the drapes had yet to be pulled. I opened the door a crack, letting a sliver of daybreak slip in. The only thing I saw were the specs of dust drifting in the beam of yellow light. I tripped over the welcome mat. I made out the sofa. It was pea-green, a quilted style with circular buttons in the cushion centers. Mr. wing-tipped shoes was no longer in sight.

I crept up the stairs and snuck back into my room. I walked over to the window, pulled back the heavy taupe blinds and looked out at the view. The ocean water was calm, nothing but a few small boats rocking around. I sat on the window ledge and stared off to sea. *It's a million dollar view*, my father had said after he'd crashed down my duffel bag on the luggage rack on the first day we'd arrived. Father had smiled deep and rocked back and forth on his heels, staring hard at the view and shaking his head with a dumbfounded grin. *The same view that the Kennedys have from their compound*, he'd said. There may have even been a tear in the old man's eye, yet I would never know, for sitting there on the ledge all I could see was the newspaper girl.

TENNIS ANYONE?

"C'mon sport, one match won't hurt you," Father said.

I groaned. "Tennis is a bore. Hitting a ball over a net? Makes me dizzy watching that fuzzy yellow comet fly back and forth," I said. "Besides Father, anyone can play tennis. Any upper-crust, narcissistic, pain in the ass can play the game."

"I suppose you're right, Jack," Father laughed.

"Jack, watch your language," Mother said, dipping the end of her napkin into her water glass and reaching over to flatten my cowlick. I shrugged her away.

"Yeah, watch your language, dipshit," said Thomas.

I flicked a piece of scrambled egg at him from across the table, then turned back toward my father.

"I don't want to do the things that any one of them can do," I said. "I want to do the very things they can't."

Maybelle arrived at our table. "More coffee, Mr. Sullivan?" she said.

"Please, Mayelle," Father said.

"May*belle*," I said, then coughed into my fist.

"May*belle*," Father said, burning his eyes into my forehead.

Father slurped his coffee as Maybelle walked away. "Didn't realize you were so familiar with the help, Jack," he said. He shook out his napkin, then threw it down on the table like a crumpled paper ball.

"I heard her introducing herself to Mr. Frederick this morning," I said, tugging on my tie and sipping water as it dribbled down my chin.

"Pardon me," said a full-figured blonde with a white polo shirt and a kelly green tennis skirt.

What a nice interruption, I thought as I stood to greet her. Thomas rushed to stand before me, banging into the table and sending the water glasses knocking against one another. Thomas was many things, older, smarter, stronger, but the one thing he wasn't was suave. He was too cocky to be suave. Overconfident, that's what Thomas was, and I muffled my laughs to watch Mr. Pre-Med Harvard's lumbering body fall into the young lady.

"I was wondering if either of you would care to join me for some mid-morning tennis? The court here is quite nice," she said.

"I would love to play tennis," I said as Thomas rolled his eyes. Father smirked in disgust.

"And I'll be free for a match tomorrow," Thomas said. "Have a bit of studies to attend to, so yes, Jack should take my place this morning."

"You know Harvard," Father said. "They never give their top students a break!"

"Harvard?" she said. "Why, Daddy wore crimson too." She turned toward me, scanning me with the bluest of blue eyes. "And you, Jack? Harvard bound?"

"Perhaps," I said. "Perhaps. But first, I'm court bound with a charming young lady named?" I stood, taking her hand.

"Isabelle Whitney," she said, curling her chin to her chest like a kitten and blushing the color of her father's alma mater.

"Isabelle Whitney, it is a true pleasure," I said. "Mother, Father, I'll see you at lunchtime." I stopped after a few feet and turned back toward the table. "Oh, and Thomas? Study hard." His lips snarled as he reached for his water glass and slurped down a few miserable gulps.

I led Isabelle to her table where proper introductions to her family were made, then excused myself to dress in my tennis whites. Once dressed, I cursed my way down the hill, angry that I'd sunken to the level of the people around me, the human puppets pulled by the strings of the elitist code. Yet, on I walked to meet sweet Isabelle courtside for a tiresome match, a match meant for a person like Thomas, where he might share his witty Cambridge stories. A match surely not fit for me, but one in which I didn't fail to entertain.

MARTINI LUNCH

Back at the Honeysuckle, couples retreated to the pool. Of course, the beach was a mere stroll over the dunes, but poolside meant service, and service meant cocktails.

When I returned for an icy shower after tennis with Isabelle, I resigned to the idea that tennis might be the only thing to help me pass the time while stuck with my family in the sixteen bedroom mansion. I ran upstairs, pulling off my shirt as I entered my room. Scolded, I was, by the Innkeeper, Ms. Gardenia.

"Gardenia, did you say?" I said when she introduced herself in a tone sharper than the sounds of a badly tuned piano.

"*Gardenia.* Gar-deen-ee-YAH!" she said, small balls of spit forming on her lips as she spoke.

This had to be a joke, I thought. Was this woman faking her last name for the sake of her Inn, her flower drenched, putrid, cold as hell Inn?

"Shirts remain on unless in the comfort of your own room, Mr. Sullivan," said Ms. Gardenia, her knobby knuckled finger wagging in front of me.

"Yes, ma'am," I said, pulling my shirt down over my head and cringing as the wrinkles around her black mustache hairs twitched when I tucked in my shirt.

Ms. Gardenia gave me the creeps. She wore long, silk bathrobes over her bathing suit and shuffled around the Inn all day sucking on cigarettes the way a baby sucks on a bottle. Her hair was frizzy and sprung out all over the place. It must have been jet black at one time, but now it was streaked with white and gray, making her look like a real skunk. I feared that going to sleep would be difficult, that I would wake up in a cool sweat and see the old maid hovering over my bed staring down at me. I shivered at the thought.

I tried to erase her image from my head as I blasted the shower water. I drenched my head, feeling the salty sweat sting my eyes as it washed its way down my face. My thoughts turned to Isabelle Whitney. Surely, she could rid my mind of the noxious moth ball scent that pulsed from Ms. Gardenia's flaky skin, or the stubbly black hairs that poked out of her chin. Isabelle Whitney's skin was smooth and golden, and when I'd walked her back to the Inn after tennis, she'd smelled far from the scent of a perfumed flower. No, Isabelle Whitney had smelled of sweet, musky sweat and I found myself rather enjoying her bouquet.

I closed my eyes and let the water pound my back. Ms. Gardenia's trembling finger, and the gray line of spit that stretched between her lips when she spoke, crept back into my mind. I tried to think about what I might be doing had I gone camping in the Adirondacks with Johnny Stewart, yet all I could imagine were Isabelle Whitney's plump breasts bouncing up and down as she hustled across the tennis court.

I turned off the shower and slung a towel around my waist, then went searching for one of the cigarettes I'd hidden in my bag. What a jerk I am, I thought. For one, I had made lousy tennis serves on purpose so Isabelle Whitney would have to charge around the court breathless and bouncing about. And second, and most importantly, I was a traitor. Thomas should have been the one out there on the court, not me. I was not made for pastimes. To be honest, I wasn't sure what I was made for, but I knew if I didn't find out soon I'd risk morphing into one of them-one of the ones I looked down on from my window, lounging on chaises by the rectangular pool, drinking their liquid lunches to relax them for their afternoon naps.

From my window, I saw Father with a martini in one hand, a cigar in the other. I saw Mother sitting by the shallow end of the pool, her eyes glued to the pages of a novel while dipping her toes into the water.

Mother wore a floppy straw hat and red sunglasses that were big and round as saucers. The other women splashed around in the pool, bobbing about like apples, their saggy middle-aged bodies crammed into pastel bikinis. They were loud and laughing and yelling out at the men, each one of them begging for attention like a bum begging for a coin. Mother seemed isolated from the other women, and for the first time when I looked at her amongst company, I wondered if she were isolating herself on purpose. I wondered if she had always isolated herself in the company of superficial women and I had never taken any notice.

Mother had grown up with elite blood beating through her veins. She was well-read, well-travelled, a Vassar graduate. A thoroughbred, my father liked to brag to the men who came over to the house for Friday night poker in the den. Sometimes, after mother had gone to sleep, Thomas and I would sneak out of our beds and lay on our bellies on the brown shag carpet in the hall outside the den. We would stay there for hours, eavesdropping on their drunken card-playing nonsense. Their jokes were off-color and though I didn't know what they were about in context, I knew who they were about: Blacks, 'spics, Jews, broads, and the occasional moan and groan about someone's own wife. I never heard Father say anything crass about Mother; I only remember the thoroughbred part. But the jokes he laughed at, the jokes he told with more gusto then he'd ever used when speaking to me about anything, those jokes I heard and goddamit, I remembered. My stomach would twist and turn as I snuck back into my bed, nauseated by the loud, slurring man who I'd heard make horrific fun of other people, the man who was my father, my father who glowed with smiles at church each Sunday and publicly shook the hands of the people he privately belittled, all the while beaming and sharing peace with each and every one of them. This man, my father, I knew then that he was a stranger to me.

Father was loud; Mother was anything of the sort. Mother was collected, even-keeled. She never raised her voice a notch; she seemed a bit too skittish for that. Mother was the peacemaker, always trying to bring our voices to a lull. But she was fierce in other ways. She was fierce in her love of family, and in her values. Not a night went by that I wasn't told I love you, not one gift was received for which I didn't write a thank-you card, and for every one of my wrong doings, I was held justly accountable. She was fierce in her passion for literature, for reading the classics, and for understanding them. And she was fierce in her love of photographs.

Mother's eyes lit up very few times. Most often, her eyes had a glassy shade pulled down in front of them. But when the shade went up, and there was light in her eyes, they were beautiful; she was beautiful, happy even. Her eyes came to life when she saw Thomas or me, always. They sparkled when she held a book in front of her. They radiated when she looked at photographs, hers or anyone else's. Mother loved capturing moments, and as with her literature, she loved understanding the moment. Even the understanding that sprung from her imagination fed into her magical bedtime stories. For the life and the love that photographs brought to my mother, I loved each one of them, too.

Lately, Father had been chiding Mother. As I eyed her distance from him at the pool, I wondered if this was also new or just new to my sense of awareness. Father nagged that she was like a wet rag, had lost her spark. *Where's the fun girl who used to take the train from Poughkeepsie and meet me in the city?* he would say, squeezing her middle as she ran around the kitchen to put dinner on the table. She would roll her eyes, swat his hand away, dish hearty servings onto our plates, then stand by her seat nibbling on the roasted turkey skin, dipping it into the gravy, licking her fingers, and gulping her wine before rushing to wash the dirty pots and pans, scrub the stove, wipe the damp hair from her face with the back of her hand, then refill her glass.

My thoughts of Mother were interrupted by a gentle tapping sound. "Hello?" the nimble voice chirped through the wooden door. I turned from the window and opened the door, forgetful that I only had only a towel around my waist. Isabelle Whitney stared a moment too long before batting her eye lids and fixing her gaze on the floor.

She took a soft breath. "Jack, would you like to join me by the pool?" she said, brushing her fingertips across her collarbone. "Daddy said we could have a cocktail. He's sure no one would notice."

"Let's do that, Isabelle," I said. "Wait for me in the main room while I get dressed?"

"Wonderful," she said, raising her shoulders high up to her ears, and swinging her ponytail from side to side.

"If we're lucky, maybe Daddy will make us a martini," she said with a playful wink.

"Boy, who doesn't love a martini?" I said.

Isabelle retreated to the main room. I dressed for the afternoon in seersucker shorts, a navy blue polo shirt, and my worn leather boat shoes. I smoked a quick cigarette while standing in front of the bathroom mirror. I glared at myself the entire time.

"You're an asshole," I said to myself, staring down the imposter in front of me. I took the last drag and flicked the butt into the toilet bowl. Then I went downstairs to meet Isabelle for the poolside martini that I would later spill into the grass and fill with water because I couldn't stomach the taste.

THE CLOTHES MAKE THE MAN

"Thank you, Maybelle," Father said as she served his eggs Benedict.

"You're welcome, Mr. Sullivan," she said.

"Oh, Harv, please. You can call me Harv," he said.

"Yes, Mr. Sullivan," she said.

Father smiled and I suspected he thought Maybelle was maintaining her respect for him by still referring to him in the proper form. He grinned and nodded while raising his eyebrows across the table at Mother. I was beginning to sense my father liked feeling respected, but not in an earned respected kind of way, rather in an expected respect kind of way, an entitled to respect kind of way. And in my eyes, hell, that was the worst kind, because that entitlement seemed to stem from only one thing, the desire to be powerful. And sitting at that table covered with fine china and crystal, being served eggs Benedict by a petite black woman, bumping elbows with New England socialites, my father thought that he was some sort of demi-god. Little did he know that I understood Maybelle. Maybelle was smarter than my father could ever hope to be and in ways my father couldn't understand. Maybelle would never refer to my father as *Harv* because Maybelle would not have a bone in her body that would desire to be on familiar terms with a man as gloating as him. Maybelle knew better. My father did not.

"Maybelle, these are my boys, Thomas and Jack. And of course you've seen my wife before," he said.

"Yes, of course, Mr. Sullivan. Hello boys, pleasure to meet you," Maybelle said, nodding at each of us. "Mr. Sullivan? Does your wife have a name like the boys do?"

Oh, Maybelle. Oh, Jesus, Maybelle. If I could make money grow on trees, well I think I would plant you a forest. Father's annoying facial tic surfaced beneath his left eye. He cleared his throat. Thomas dropped his head as if in prayer. I looked at Mother who raised her chin a bit higher and sipped her water.

"Of course, of course. Claire, her name is Claire," Father said.

"Pleasure to meet you, Mrs. Claire Sullivan," said Maybelle as she added more coffee to Mother's cup, then waltzed away.

Father eyed his half-empty cup and turned his head to watch Maybelle gliding over to the next table. Lines of confusion seeped deep into his forehead. He shook his head fast like he was trying to get water out of his ear, then filled his chest with a deep breath of air and set the cup down.

Father cleared his throat. "Thomas, you'll be playing tennis with the Whitney girl this afternoon," he said.

"Yes, sir," Thomas said, sitting up straight as if he had won the prize. It wasn't a prize I much minded loosing. I'd had my fair share of Isabelle Whitney yesterday, including the vomit that she'd spewed all over me after too many cocktails. Perhaps Thomas would have better luck.

Father cleared his throat. "Very well then. She is a nice Southern girl, from the Carolinas. I found her quite pleasant when she stopped by the table the other day. Hope you didn't spoil her for Thomas, Jack!"

"No, Father. I don't believe I did," I said, rolling my eyes.

"Jack, you and I are taking a drive to Chatam this morning," Father said.

"Yes, Father," I said. "Mother, will you be joining us?"

"Why thank you, Jack. I'd love to," she said.

"There's a formal dinner party next weekend in the dining room, Jack. I want you to look your best. You aren't a Harvard man yet, but there's no reason why you shouldn't start looking more like one. Your hair is getting too long in the front, son. We'll find you a barber to take care of that as well," Father said, as runny egg gathered in the corner of his mouth. He chewed like a caveman, my father did. He chewed everything like he was gnawing away at some tough piece of meat that he had killed with his bare hands. Watching him grind his food like that made me want to chomp his head off.

"I favor my hair this way, Father. I won't cut it," I said.

26

"Well, I can't force you, Jack. But look around, son. We're in Hyannis Port. Do you see the Kennedys walking around with long hair? No, son. You don't."

"No, Father, I don't because I don't *see* the Kennedys. Do you? Do you see them? Are Jack and Jackie coming to the *Honeysuckle Inn* for dinner this weekend? I doubt it. I'll be waiting in the car to go to Chatam. I'll let you buy me a new dinner coat. You can dress me up in your hand picked clothes like your personal puppet and pull my strings all night long in front of the other guests at the dinner party, but my hair stays the way it is."

Father leaned forward on his elbows, positioning his fork and knife in either hand. "Well, I'm glad about the clothes, son. The clothes make the man, you know." He looked around the table and laughed as though he had said something particularly innovative. "And Jack, you never know who will show up at this dinner party. *Hyannis Port*, son. We're in Hyannis Port now. We are neighbors with the President and his family, Jack. You even share his name. You have to be prepared should your paths cross. And don't forget he was a Harvard man, Jack. *Harvard*. Why is it that Thomas understands what I'm talking about and you can't make sense of a single word? Now, let's rethink that haircut, shall we?"

I walked outside and circled around the Studebaker, giving a swift kick to the rear tire. My old man's delusional, I thought. I had a quack for a father; wasn't that just great? My father actually believed that President John F. Kennedy was going to stroll through the doors of Ms. Gardenia's low brow upper-class Inn.

And Thomas? Why does Thomas understand you? I thought. For the same reason Thomas used to snicker at the filthy, racist, ignorant jokes you and your pals spewed about in our den every Friday night. While I lay sleepless in the twin bed next to Thomas, talking to God in my head about everything I had heard and tried to make sense of that came from my only role model of a man, Thomas snored away, happy as clam, in the bed next to me. That's why.

My parents came out to the car at long last. I slouched in the back seat and scowled out the window. If clothes truly made the man, and my father was in charge of choosing mine for a dinner party, then I should have known as I later stood in a men's shop in Chatam with a sales woman shoving a tape measure into my balls, that my fate looked as foul as the dead fish that washed up on the Hyannis Port shore.

*****

"It's called the Honey Bowl," Father said as we drove back to the Inn from our Chatam shopping excursion.

"The *what*?" I said.

"The Honey Bowl! Imagine it, Jack! All the fathers and sons are gathered on the back lawn of the Honeysuckle. The ocean's behind us. We're all playing football like a family, the other men are like uncles, the young sons like cousins. I bet Isabelle Whitney will be there, huh sport? Rooting you on in one hell of a cheerleader sweater! Hell, all the women can cheer us on, and there'll be sandwiches waiting for us after the game. You could almost picture a similar scene playing out at the Kennedy compound, couldn't you? But, it will be *us,* Jack. It will be *our* family. Ah, the Honey Bowl. Fantastic, isn't it?"

"Super," I said, rolling my eyes. Mother looked back at me from the front seat and smiled, then chuckled against her hand.

"I told them you play quarterback, sport," Father said. "All the men and boys will play. Ms. Gardenia said it's a Honeysuckle Inn summertime tradition. And here we are a proud part of it. Ain't that swell?"

"Oh, yeah. Real swell," I said as Mother tried harder to muffle her laughter. She pressed both hands flat against her mouth, shook her head, and tried not to look back at me. But soon enough she'd lost all control and her stifled laughs turned into sharp yowls. She began fanning her face, flushed a scarlet red. She bent over at the waist and pounded her feet into the floor. And wouldn't you know but while watching mother like that, a slow laugh began to churn in the pit of my stomach, itching its way up under my rib cage and into my chest until it exploded straight out of my mouth.

"What's so funny, Claire?" Father said, his fingers flexing around the steering wheel.

"Oh, I don't know. Nothing. It's nothing," she said, waving her hand, then bursting into a deeper laugh that seemed to be propelled from the depths of her body until she was clutching the dashboard and trying to catch breaths in between her hysterics.

"What *is* it, Claire?" father said between gritted teeth. His hands clenched the wheel, his knuckles white as a smoke.

"I mean, c'mon Harv, the Honey Bowl? The *Honey* Bowl?" Tears flew from her eyes. She rolled down the window and popped out her head. "Oh boy, that's a good one. I need some air," she said, bursting into random fits of laughter the whole way home, the kind of laughter that comes when you know you're supposed to be quiet and that just makes it all the more worse, like in school, or in church, or in the car with Father frothing at the mouth over some Hyannis Port wet dream of his called the Honey Bowl.

The ride back was long, what with Mother and I trying to stop ourselves from laughing and Father looking like a kettle ready to blow its whistle. When we pulled into the drive at the Honeysuckle, Father looked in the backseat and said, "You'll join us on the field tomorrow, won't you sport?" I nodded, opened the door and stretched. The three of us walked toward the Inn.

"Sure thing," I said, then made an imaginary football pass at him which perked his spirits and sent him running backward across the lawn yelling, "I'm going long! I'm going long!"

A pair of men with golf clubs slung over their shoulders also made their way from the driveway to the Inn. They cheered on Father and then one called out, "And the crowd goes wild!"

Father looked like he'd won the Heisman. He gave me two thumbs-up for making him shine in front of the crowd. The men whacked each other's back, grinning like baboons. I escorted Mother inside.

THE LETTERMAN

"Good morning, Maybelle," I said, hustling downstairs and shoving my arms into my navy blue blazer.

"Why, hello, Jack," Maybelle said. "I was just coming to knock on your door. Your father's been expecting you to join the family for breakfast. Have to get a hearty meal in you if you're going to play in the Honey Bowl."

I stopped to straighten my red striped tie in the hall mirror, rolling my eyes all the while.

"Oh, don't be a spoiled sport now; you'll play like the rest of them," she said, ushering me ahead of her toward the stairwell.

"Maybelle?" I said, stopping on the landing and turning to face her. "Ever in a million years would you want to spend your afternoon sitting on the grass cheering for a bunch of overweight men on the verge of a mid-life crisis as they drooled and panted their way all over the back lawn pretending to be the Kennedy brothers?"

"Why, no. No, now I wouldn't." She crossed her arms and jutted out her hip.

I jogged down the steps, landing with a thud on the wooden floor. "Well, I sure as hell don't want to spend my afternoon playing football with them." I spit in my hand and pressed my palm against the front pieces of hair sticking straight up off the front of my head.

Maybelle strode down the steps and walked straight pass me. She turned and centered her feet, laced up tight in white pump heels, on a worn spot on the floor. The wood where she stood was discolored, a creamy caramel circle that faded into a shiny dark brown stain. She pulled back the French doors that opened to the dining room, and extended her hand, signaling for me to move forward.

"Never in a million years," she chuckled, shaking her head and lowering her gaze toward the floor. Then she looked back up, pressed her lips together real tight, breathed in through her nostrils, and sighed.

I raised my eyebrows and nodded, in a *now do you understand?* kind of way.

"But Jack Sullivan," she said as I took my first step past her, landing my scuffed leather shoe smack dab on the marble floor. "You and I may play for two very different teams, but we both know we're better off doing just as we're told."

"Sport! Glad you could join us!" Father called from his table.

I hung my head low and walked over to my seat. Maybelle came over moments later with a steaming plate of scrambled eggs, two quarter size hotcakes, and three thick slices of Canadian bacon. She even took the time to drizzle warm maple syrup over the food.

"Thank you, ma'am," I said.

"You're very welcome, Jack. You'll need your energy for out on the field today," she said.

"Maybelle, I'll have you know that Jack is a varsity letterman," Father said.

"Is that right? Well now, I figured him as one to know all the rules of the game," she said.

"And what a game it is," I said.

"You'll join the ladies at the field, Maybelle? Cheer on us old boys!" Father said.

"Oh, Mr. Sullivan, I wouldn't miss it in a million years," she said, refilling his coffee cup and waltzing away.

There was something quite magnetic about Maybelle Winson. I believed she held the secrets of the world; she seemed to have that sense about her. And she did show up to the football game. She brought out large weaved picnic baskets overflowing with food from the kitchen: roasted turkey sandwiches spread with cranberry preserves and thin layers of stuffing, salami, cheese and crackers, cans of pop and cold bottles of beer. She spread out large quilts that the ladies positioned themselves on. She laid out hand towels on a small wooden bench for us to wipe the sweat off our brows. She poured cups of water in neat little rows so we wouldn't go thirsty. Then Maybelle returned to the Inn and was replaced by Ms. Gardenia.

Old lady Gardenia wore a midnight blue wool cardigan sweater with a white block letter Y on the large right side square pocket, no matter that it was the middle of July and the heat was stifling. The sweater looked real raggedy. There were gray pilled balls covering the white block letter and I wondered where she'd scored the damn thing. Ms. Gardenia taught the women cheers, and they all stood and yelled for this one or that one to *Score!* I rolled my eyes.

I did end up playing quarterback, but just like on the tennis court with Isabelle Whitney, I couldn't stop myself from throwing real lousy passes. I couldn't help but want to make the men, clones of my father, sweat it out a bit. Part of me wanted to humiliate them, right there with their wives and daughters looking on all hopeful and bright. Terrible of me, I know, but it was the truth. I wanted to make the men think they could grasp the football. I wanted to bring them as I close as I could to the brown leather hide skin. I wanted them to feel the ball against their fingertips for a mere second before fumbling their footing in the grass and losing their spotty balance. I wanted to sack their dream of catching a pass and making any sort of play, let alone a touchdown. Most of all, I wanted to take away their pride.

And as I caught sight of Isabelle Whitney jumping up in down, cheering on her father, in yes, what was one hell of a cheerleader sweater, I saw the glimmer of hope in her eyes too. Her hands were clasped in prayer against her mouth, wanting for her father the very thing I wished to take away as the wisps of his silver hair scattered in the wind and he raced down the field with his arms wide open, waiting for my letterman worthy pass.

I couldn't help but to remember that this crazed looking man, hungry to sink his teeth into the ball and be carried off the field dripping sweet with the smell of Honeysuckle victory, that this was the same man who had spoon fed martinis to Isabelle days before by the pool. And I hated him for that, for bringing out in Isabelle a girl who slurred, turned sloppy, and lost all of her previous lady-like charm. A girl who had vomited all over me behind the pool cabana, where we'd snuck a few smokes, and to whom I'd felt responsible for escorting back to her room for fear that if she stayed by the pool she'd be fed more martinis, or worse yet, she'd wind up floating face down in the pool without anyone taking notice.

And so I'd escorted Isabelle back to the Inn that drunken night, where I brought her to her room and turned on the lights as she banged into a lamp, sending it crashing to the ground, leaving me to clean up the shattered bulb because God knows Isabelle would have sliced her fingers to pieces picking up the shards in her state. And as she'd drooped down into a chair and kicked her shoes off across the floor, I used the bathroom to wash off her vomit that was stuck to my arm, half-gagging and half-hiccupping because I was in rare form myself. And my polo shirt, once white, was spotted with clumps of orange, so I'd taken that off too and threw it in the wastebasket, glad that my undershirt had been spared too much damage. And Isabelle, I'd found her toothbrush and called her in by the sink. Hell, I'd even helped her brush her teeth. She'd laughed and giggled and rolled her head back as she spit out the mint toothpaste and it dribbled out of her mouth. I'd wiped her chin and took the tiny tortoise shell barrettes out of her hair, leaving them in a cluster under the mirror. And then, when I'd gone to squeeze by her to prepare her bed, wouldn't you know that Isabelle Whitney did her kittenish thing again. She'd curled her chin to her chest, and let her soft curls just slide down around her eyes, before peeking up at me through the part in her hair and batting her long, thick lashes.

"Isabelle, I think it's time for you to go to bed," I'd said.

She'd nuzzled herself up into my chest just like a cat and began making all of these little purring sounds and saying things like, "Please, don't go, Jack. I'm too drunk to sleep alone. Please sleep here with me in case I get sick during the night and throw up again." She'd slouched down on the floor and curled up in a ball.

"I've heard stories about people being sick in their sleep from having too much drink in them, and the next thing you know someone finds them the next day, and they're dead. Dead, Jack! Please, don't leave me alone tonight. I don't want to go like one of them." Her purrs had turned to whimpers.

"*Shh*," I'd said as I pulled her up beside me. Her forehead had flopped against her knees and little sniffles escaped her. "Don't cry, Isabelle. Don't cry. It'll be alright."

She'd looked up at me, the saddest, most helpless look I'd ever seen. And then little tears, little dew drop tears, just started flowing from her eyes. "Please don't leave me, Jack. Please, Jack."

And the next thing I knew there I was sleeping scrunched up in the armchair next to Isabelle Whitney's bed and using a bath towel as a blanket. And you know something? She did vomit that night, all night. And once I'd awoken to the sound of her choking on her vomit in bed, half-asleep. And as I cleaned her up, and slid a towel between her and the soiled sheet, that old bastard's face kept flashing in front of mine. What if I hadn't slept in her room that night? What if Isabelle had choked on her own martini puke and died in her bed?

"Jack! Jack! I'm open!" Mr. Whitney called, waving his arms over his head, and snapping me out of my thoughts.

I fired the ball, aiming to skim the old man's fingertips. Oh, he thought he had it. Why for a split second he was reliving his glory days playing for Harvard. In that single moment he was the strapping young buck with a gaggle of women screaming his name, their falsies knocking about. And now he was the envy of all the men on the field and off because this would be the game point and the end zone was just a few steps behind him.

Mr. Whitney arched his body sideways, stretching his limbs out as far as they would go. But the ball was just shy of him and the old man wasn't as agile as he'd once been. With the plunk of the ball against the plush grass behind him, the good ol' Mr. Whitney tripped backward over his feet, his wide ass landing in the end zone, his legs spread eagle in front of him, and his arms empty handed.

The other team gathered in a circle hooting and hollering and Ms. Gardenia in her raggedy old Yale sweater bustled out onto the field with an empty honey pot full of flowers as the trophy. Isabelle Whitney criss-crossed her arms over her chest and frowned upon the scene as Mrs. Whitney rushed over to help up Mr. Whitney. The men on my team ran over to Mr. Whitney as well. Father slapped me on the back and said, "Good try, Jack. It was very close."

Mr. Whitney hobbled over toward me with one hand gripping his lower back. "Damn sorry I didn't catch your pass, son," he said, straightening up and extending his hand.

"It was a solid effort, sir," I said, returning the handshake.

I shook hands with the other men and excused myself to shower.

"Jack?" Mr. Whitney said, trotting behind me.

"Sir?" I said.

He stopped and put his hands on his hips. He breathed heavy through his teeth. "There's a clambake on the beach at five. Would you escort Isabelle?"

"It would be my pleasure." I lied through my teeth.

"Atta boy, Jack!" He jogged backward, then shook his pointer finger in the air. "I'll even make you kids some *martinis*. Huh? How about that?"

I looked around the field to see if anybody else had been listening.

He waved his hand at me as if to say, *Ah, go on*!

"My Isabelle loves her martinis!" he said, raising his eyebrows up and down.

I nodded and turned to make my way back to the Inn. My lousy pass hadn't changed a goddamn thing about the fact that Mr. Whitney overfed sweet Isabelle martinis. Back inside my bathroom, I lay in the empty bathtub in my football clothes, chain smoking cigarettes and flicking ashes over the tub's edge and onto the marble floor.

ON BEALS STREET

I climbed over the dunes and headed toward the terrific glow of the bonfire, but not before dropping a few cans of beer in the sand beneath an abandoned lawn chair. On most days the narrow stretch of private beach in front of the Honeysuckle was sparse, sprinkled with just a few sunbathers or beachcombers. Today, it seemed like the whole Inn was gathered on the sand. I kind of liked the sight.

Ms. Gardenia had hired some local men to come by and put a clam bake together. They were a friendly bunch, singing songs about *chowdah* as they shucked the clams. Everyone huddled in groups, chattering away about nothing. Folding tables were set up on the beach, covered with some of the best looking food I'd seen since we'd arrived in Hyannis Port.

My mouth watered as I scouted out what food looked best and waited for the moment old lady Gardenia rang the dinner bell and I could sink my teeth into the food. There was a large pot of simmering clam chowder that looked creamy and rich. Two men were steaming littlenecks and I could already taste the chewy clams in my mouth, why I even imagined the flavor of sand in the clam shell, having always savored that authentic gritty taste. Corn on the cob, bright yellow as a honeybee, was laid out on a platter. Further down the table were bowls of salt potatoes, coleslaw, dinner rolls as puffy as my goose down pillow, and lo and behold, there were piles of bright red lobsters just calling out for their shells to be cracked and their tasty meat to be drenched in butter.

Off on another table, Ms. Gardenia had set up a makeshift bar with a younger man, who looked no older than Thomas, serving up the drinks. The fellow wore a red sport coat and green plaid shorts and looked nervous as hell to be waiting on the evening's crowd. Speaking of Thomas, he was already getting cozy with Isabelle Whitney, a thought that made me feel a little nervous myself. After all, Mr. Whitney had asked me to be Isabelle's escort for the evening, and I had said yes. I strolled over to where the two of them sat and tried to make small talk.

"Daddy paid off the bartender. Looks like we'll get drinks as we want them!" she said, doing a little shimmy in her seat as the straps of her madras beach dress slipped down her tanned shoulder.

I raised my eyes and smirked. That's great, I thought. Now I'd have to babysit Isabelle another night.

"Tell me more about Harvard, Tommy," Isabelle gushed, clasping her hands under her chin and leaning up against Thomas.

"Oh, Isabelle," he said, extending his arm behind her back and resting it on her chair. "It's an institution for only our nation's finest. Anyone who associates with a Harvard man is considered the belle of the ball. No finer treatment is bestowed upon a lady, than on the lady joined by a Harvard man." He moved his drink in a slow clockwise circle, letting the ice cubes clink against the glass while he grinned his shit-eating grin and took a long, slow swig.

This was going to be a long night, I thought. I looked around in every direction to see what other table had a free chair I might occupy. My thoughts were interrupted by Ms. Gardenia rattling a bronze bell in the air. "Come and get it!" she sang.

And boy did I. My paper plate overflowed with lobster and coleslaw and two ears of corn. Butter trickled down my fingers as I smothered the salt potatoes. I poured a few extra splashes onto my plate for the lobster.

Everyone scurried to fill up their plates. They gathered around the small square tables and sat on the lumpy yellow cushions. Thomas and Isabelle sat pressed together with his arm still draped behind her back. I sat on the bench across from them while two Cornell sophomores filled the other seats. Their presence relieved me. At least I would have company in my misery as I sat witnessing the naïve Isabelle fawn over a goon like Thomas. We rattled on with stories about Ithaca, the crappy winters, the gray skies, and then we all thanked god that at least we had hockey.

"Where do you go?" the red headed one said.

"Oh, I've got one year of high school left, applications go out next fall," I said.

"To the Ivys?" he said.

"Of course to the Ivys," Thomas sneered.

Isabelle nodded like she knew. "Oh, of course. Of course Jack will go to Harvard. I just know it," she said.

My body went warm inside. She was sweet, Isabelle Whitney was. Poor thing was a little stuck on Thomas at the moment though. She was blinded by that crimson light. But hell, she wouldn't be the last one to fall ill to that fate.

Thomas excused himself to get a beer.

"Tommy?" Isabelle murmured in his ear, gliding her arm across his shoulder, and nuzzling his neck like she'd done to me before. "Tommy, bring me back a martini, won't you?"

"Yes, sweetheart," he said, rolling his eyes at the Cornell guys when Isabelle wasn't looking. The guys laughed and Isabelle gave a small smile, perhaps not knowing what on earth she was smiling about. Then she shook her head and bent it forward, covering her mouth and giggling up a storm. I dug into my dinner like I was searching for gold. I couldn't look at Isabelle. Her liquor was setting in and she had that wild look in her eye.

"*Jack*," she cooed across the table. The Cornell men shot one another a look. The red head coughed into his hand, the other guy gave a snort and corn flew out of his mouth. They picked up their empty plates, gave a wave, and left the table just as Isabelle Whitney's foot slid up my leg and landed smack dab in my lap.

"Excuse me, Isabelle, but it seems Thomas is your escort for the evening," I said.

"Oh, silly me. I suppose you're right," she said, gliding her foot back down to the ground.

Thomas returned, dropping down hard into his seat and sending the whole table shaking. He set down Isabelle's drink, then leaned in to light the cigarette pressed between her glossy lips.

I excused myself and hunted down Mr. Whitney.

"Sir," I said when I found him hovering around the bar. "Sir, it seems that Isabelle and my brother, Thomas, are enjoying one another's company. If you don't mind, I think he'd like to be her escort this evening."

"Why Jack, I appreciate you sharing that information with me. Very well, then. Perhaps next time. Must be the old Harvard connection! Daddy's little girl looking for someone like her old man!"

"Must be," I said, shrugging.

"Don't fret, Jack. Get yourself accepted at Harvard and you'll have your pick of the litter, too. Just like your brother."

"Yes, sir." I turned and watched Isabelle wobbling alongside Thomas toward the bonfire.

The sky was darkening. Clusters of people scattered along the beach. Shadows grew along the sand. A group of childrens' cherub faces illuminated behind the bonfire. Their hands were half-covered by their sweatshirt sleeve cuffs as they held onto their parents' hands. I spotted Mother and Father with a few other familiar faces, all smiling and laughing. I made my way over to see what all the fun was about.

"Hiya, Jackie!" Father said, roughing up my hair.

"Hi there," I said, trying to smooth down my cowlick.

"So as I was saying," Father's voice boomed. I stuffed my hands deep into my pockets and looked around the circle. The only one to acknowledge me with a smile was Mother. The rest of them were mesmerized by Father, all waiting for the master storyteller to continue on with his tale.

"It all began on Beals Street," Father said.

Oh shit, I thought. Conversations beginning with Beals Street only meant one thing.

"That's in Brookline, isn't that right?" said Mrs. Goldsmith.

"Brookline, indeed, Betty," Father said. "You've got a smart one there, Walt."

Walt winked at Betty.

"Yes, now, where were we? Oh yes, why we were over on Beals Street!" Father bellowed. The crowd laughed. "You see, my family lived there in the early years, at the same time the Kennedy family lived there."

The crowd hushed. Someone who lived on the same street as JFK in his childhood? Standing on a Hyannis Port beach to tell about it? The stars gleamed in their eyes.

"The President moved away when he was oh, about four years old. I was three then, so my memories are somewhat limited. But I do remember my mother saying what a nice family the Kennedys were. How well behaved the boys were. Nice Irish Catholic family at that. Why, she hoped I would behave just like one of those Kennedy boys!" Father looked up at the stars, shook his drink up to the sky, and laughed. "Hey, Mom!" he said, "I'm trying!" The others laughed along with him.

"Well, in your own way, you are, Darling," Mother said, her voice a soft breath. She slid her arm beneath his and rested her head on his shoulder, shifting the mood to a rather sincere one. She stared off into the night sky. She took a fast sip of her gin and tonic, then gave a swift nod of her head like she was about to pitch an idea to a boardroom.

"Born on Beals Street yourself, later on a Harvard man, now look at you, summering in Hyannis Port," she said. I knew those recognitions were important to my father, but didn't suspect them crucial to my mother's well-being. Frankly, I found the way that Father reached for those connections to be pathetic. Still, however Mother found them to be, she was trying to shine a light on Father in front of the crowd, and she had. He puffed his cigar three times, then pecked her on the cheek.

"Not to mention a wife as elegant as Jackie," Mr. Porter said with a wink toward Mother. Mother looked coy, but smiled like the sun had set on her. I smiled, too. She was beautiful, my mother was.

"Oh, come now, Porter! No woman's as gorgeous as Jacqueline Kennedy," Father said. "I mean Jackie Kennedy, va-va-va voom!"

Limp smiles fell around the crowd. Mother looked down at her feet and ran her toe in circles in the sand.

"Well, we're both Vassar girls to say the least," Mother said, as an even softer breath escaped her.

"To Vassar," Mr. Porter said, eyeing the crowd with expectation.

"To Vassar!" The others said, and raised their glasses high.

Mother crossed her arms over chest and ran her fingers up and down them. She turned her gaze and stared out at the ocean. Her bottom lip quivered until she clenched her teeth, turned and gave a quick upward jolt of her glass, took a fast sip, and forced a smile. Mother slid right back into conversation with the other ladies while the men reminisced about their good ol' college days. I watched Mother a moment as she spoke with the others. Her eyes were flat and lifeless. The only soul I saw in them was the reflection of the bonfire flames. I looked at my father, then down at the sand. My chest tightened so hard I thought my lungs had collapsed. There seemed to be no air. I could have sworn I was suffocating.

I broke away unnoticed, snatching the cans of beer from where I'd hid them beneath a lawn chair before walking down the beach to find a good, empty spot by the water. I hated Hyannis Port, but I hated my father more. Few women were as beautiful as Mrs. Kennedy. My mother was one of those few. Shouldn't Father have seen that in her also? Shouldn't he have glowed about her to the crowd as she had done for him?

The old man yelled down to me at the shore.

"Don't stay up too late, son! Remember, you have your Harvard interview tomorrow!" he said.

I waved my hand over my head to let him know that I'd heard him. "Yeah, yeah," I grumbled. I walked on until the bonfire was out of sight. I sank down into the sand, cracked a can open, and guzzled the flat beer. I chucked the smashed cans into the dunes behind me. When the woozy waves of inebriation set into my body, I laid back until I felt the coarse sand against my neck, and I fell asleep.

It wasn't the waves rolling up the beach that woke me, nor was it my father yelling in my ear to clean myself up for the drive to Cambridge, it was a hushed voice that echoed in my ear and jabbed at my conscience until I awoke.

"Help me. Oh God, please help me," she said.

"Who's there?" I said, startling myself onto all fours.

"Please help me."

Fear tore through my body. I stumbled to my feet, tripping over clumps of seaweed. I darted the shore looking for somebody, anybody.

"Where are you?" I called through the murky light of dawn.

The cries were small like those of a broken-winged bird. I ran toward the sounds. I bolted up the dunes, crushed the twisted reeds out of the way, then felt around the earth for someone, anyone. My foot bumped against something hard, and I grasped my hand down around something soft. It was flesh on a limb.

"Help me."

I turned around and the voice was at the tip of my feet.

"I can't stand up."

And then I heard a whimper that quieted into a low purr.

"*Isabelle*?" I said, lunging down toward her. I was on all fours, pushing her matted hair out of her eyes and checking to see if the helpless girl might actually be Isabelle. Her big, round eyes locked with mine.

"Jack? Oh, Jack, thank God it's you. Help me back to the Honeysuckle, won't you, Jack?"

"Of course, Isabelle. Of course." My startled voice lulled as I scooped her up in my arms.

"What happened, Isabelle?"

"It was my legs, Jack. They were all cramped up. I couldn't stand to walk. Every time I tried, I just crashed to the ground. I felt so weak. I was so afraid. I'd been calling out for help for hours, praying that somebody would find me, anybody at all. And there you were, Jack. I'm so glad it was you. Thank you for finding me."

42

Isabelle nuzzled her head into the space between my collarbone and chin, but this time she didn't make any purring noises; this time she wept. Trudging up the hill toward the Honeysuckle, Isabelle growing heavy in my arms, I stopped to take a breath. It was then that I caught sight of the blurred silhouettes in the main room. Shit, I thought. Now what was I going to do. There was blood on Isabelle's arms, scratches like. And she couldn't even walk.

The day was breaking. The birds were chirping. The air was soft. I could make out the tops of the tall pine trees surrounding the Honeysuckle, most all else was gray. Out of the corner of my eye, I caught sight of a small flicker of light shining through the kitchen window. Maybelle, I thought. And so I picked up the pace and headed for the backdoor. Through the screen I could see Maybelle inside the kitchen doing that familiar dance from sink to stove to serving platter. I rapped on the door. She looked over sideways, then rushed toward us.

"What happened to that girl?" she said, cocking her head sideways and burning her gaze straight through my eyes.

"I don't know, Maybelle. I swear. I found her like this on the beach," I said.

She looked over her shoulder, then pushed open the screen door as she shushed the springs with her fluttering hand as they creaked. She shooed us to a space between the stove and the broom closet. "You tell me what happened to that girl, and don't you *dare* lie to me," she said with her nostrils flaring and her index finger pointed right up under my eyes.

"Ms. Winson," Isabelle mumbled. "Ms. Winson, Jack's telling you the truth, ma'am. He found me like this."

"I fell asleep on the beach last night, Maybelle. I woke up hearing someone calling out for help. I swear to it. I went searching and I found Isabelle like this," I said.

"Alright, alright. I believe you, Jack," said Maybelle, putting her arms around our backs and drawing us into a huddle. "Now listen here, the both of you. There's a couple in the front room. I'm going to distract them. While I do, Jack, you bring Miss Isabelle to the first room on the right, do you understand me? It's the maid's chambers and I have toiletries in there. I'll get Miss Isabelle bathed and have her wear a robe up to her room. It'd be a little out of character for anyone to see her in a robe. Miss. Isabelle, if anyone asks, you'll tell them that you felt ill and came down to me for some aspirin. In the meantime, Jack, it's Sunday and this is the last thing I need right now, but I'm grateful to be of help. While I'm with Miss Isabelle, I'll need you to go down and get the papers. Leave 'em right on the back porch, you hear? Don't go banging the door, I'll know to look for 'em. Alright?"

"Yes, ma'am," I said, scurrying to the maid's chambers with Isabelle.

"You'll be alright," I said.

"Thank you, Jack," Isabelle said. She sat at the foot of Maybelle's bed, right up on the edge. She stared down at the floor. One hand clutched her stomach while the other rest behind her ear, twirling a strand of hair real tight around her index finger.

"I'll see you around, Isabelle."

"Ok then, I'll see you, Jack."

I slipped out of the room, out the front door, and jogged down the driveway to my Sunday post. I circled around the mailbox a few times, kicking my feet into the dirt, stuffing my hands into my pockets and feeling anxious about the morning, Isabelle, heck, all of it.

"Jack!" a voice yelled from down the road.

I squinted into the sun to make out the vague shape. The figure came closer.

"Thomas?" I said.

"Little brother, what are you doing up so early?" He punched me on the arm and walked straight by me and toward the Honeysuckle.

"Cambridge trip today. I wanted to get some fresh air this morning, clear the nerves," I said as Thomas turned around and gave me a thumbs up. "And what about you, Thomas?"

He stopped and jogged over to me. "Gotta call it a night sometime!"

"Is that right?" I said. "And what about Isabelle?"

"I dunno. I'm sure she made it back in one piece."

"You didn't walk her back to the Inn?"

Thomas looked confused, as if the thought of escorting a girl home would have never occurred to him. "Little brother, here's some sage advice. You find a girl who likes to drink, and that Isabelle's a real lush, let me tell you. You take her to a secluded spot. Get her drunk, take all the fun you can get out of her, and then move on to meet the girls who are up for some late night conversation. You know, the smart girls, the quality ones. Now there's some food for thought, Jack. Glad I got the chance to share it with you. See you at breakfast, dipshit." He punched my arm and broke into a trot toward the Honeysuckle.

My heart started bashing around my chest. I couldn't help but smash my fist into the mailbox a few times. Cocky bastard, I thought. Guys like Thomas were what happened when ignorant men like my father told dirty jokes in the family room. Guys like Thomas were what happened when your father embarrassed your mother in front of a group of people by insisting that she didn't hold a flame to Jacqueline Kennedy. Guys like Thomas were all around me.

I jumped out of my skin as the rusted green pickup swung around the curb. I noticed the bumper had been painted white and wondered who'd taken the time to paint it.

"Papers," I said into the cloud of sand stirred up by the squealing tires. The truck halted and the newspaper girl reached out her arm, pulled up the door lever, and jumped down from the truck. The sand settled and when it did, we were face to face. She pushed a hard candy around the inside of her mouth with the tip of her tongue, then bit it between her teeth and smiled a cute, crooked smile.

"Hello," I said.

She pushed the candy deep into her cheek.

"Hiya!" she said, and I smiled to see the grape candy stain coating her front teeth.

She hopped up onto the back bumper, reached over and pulled up on the thick, knotty twine holding the paper stack.

I lunged for the pile. Before I had a chance to steady myself, she'd dropped them down into my outstretched hands.

"Morning, son," the man at the wheel called back through the small sliding window behind the driver seat as I wobbled and tried to catch my balance.

"Sir," I called back, trying to pull myself together. "Fine morning indeed."

The newspaper girl chewed on her purple lips and smiled.

"Morning," she whispered and lowered her head.

"Good morning," I said as our hands touched under the newspaper pile. Neither one of us was expecting the touch; it just kind of happened. But we left our hands against one another's for what felt like forever.

I caught sight of her father in the rearview mirror. He stared at me from underneath his greasy baseball cap.

"Time to go, Jenny!" he barked, scratching his head with the rim of his cap, and leaning his forearm against the wheel.

"Yes, Daddy," she said, locking eyes with me and walking backward until her backside bumped up against the truck.

I smiled and kind of laughed. She turned red as tomato sauce and hurried over to the passenger door, tucking her hair behind her ear and giggling. She pushed the door handle down and hopped up on the seat. Her hand gripped the top of the door ready to heave it shut.

I let the papers crash to the ground in a heap and reached out for the door. I gave it a gentle slam shut, rapped my hand twice along the top, nodded my head, and said, "You both have a nice day."

"Thank you, son. Give Maybelle our best," her father said.

"Will do, sir," I said.

The newspaper girl slid her hand over the door. She wore one of those dime store mood rings on her second finger. The color at the moment was a deep turquoise blue.

"I'm Jenny," she said.

"Hi, Jenny," I said, captivated by the brown freckles on the bridge of her nose.

Her father shifted into drive before I could say another thing, and the truck sped off.

"I'm Jack!" I yelled out after the green flash bolting down the road.

Jenny stuck her long ballerina arm out the window and waved as the sound of my name whirled in the wind.

ADMISSIONS

I sipped my orange juice and took a bite of rye toast. I couldn't stomach much else. Must have been my nerves.

"We'll see you this evening, Darling. Don't wait on us for dinner. I'm not sure what time we'll be back from Cambridge," Mother said.

Father stood by the table and pecked Mother on the cheek. "And you're sure you don't mind traveling without me, Claire?"

"No, Darling. Anyway, I'll have Jack with me." She cupped my chin in her hand and excused herself to get a scarf for her hair.

"Son, I want you to knock the socks off of the Admissions Director. Do you hear me?" Father said. "And remember, Jack, you're a Sullivan. You are meant to be at Harvard."

"Yes, Father," I said, standing up to shake his hand.

Thomas didn't look up or say good-bye. He just devoured his food like a pig at its trough.

"So long, Thomas," I said.

Thomas grunted. Father sat back down. I pushed my chair away from the table, and headed for the door, passing by the Whitney's table on my way out. Mr. Whitney stood.

"Give 'em hell, Jack!" Mr. Whitney said, putting one hand on my arm and slapping my back.

"Yes, sir, I will," I laughed.

From her seat, Isabelle sat up pin-straight and fluttered her eyes at me. "Good luck at Harvard, Jack."

"Thank you, Isabelle. Have a nice day here at the Honeysuckle."

"Oh, I will, Jack," she said, smiling. "The sun is shining, the beach is calling, the day is getting brighter by the minute," she chirped like a bird.

"That's real great. Have fun then."

Her face softened. Her shoulders relaxed. "Thank you, Jack."

I smiled and nodded. I knew what the thank you was all about. Isabelle Whitney, a sweet girl she was.

Mother waited for me by the Studebacker. Inside the car, the air was real thick. We both cranked our windows down. I folded back the sleeves of my blue button-down shirt and loosened my tie. The blazer Father had bought for me in Chatam lay across the backseat.

Mother and I drove down Route 6, taking in the small town scenery of the Cape. The day felt quiet. Few cars drove along the road and fewer people were out walking. The clouds rolled by like gray barrels and all of a sudden it began to drizzle. I watched an old woman zip inside a market, a newspaper covering her head. A wiry brown dog yelped as a young man tied it's leash to a bike rack. The man hopped over puddles and into the market, shaking his coat dry with a smile as he waved to someone through the window. Kind of felt sorry for the mangy beast, didn't seem like his owner was too concerned about him sitting out there on the pavement getting all cold and wet.

I looked over at Mother. She stared straight ahead. Her eyes were fixed on the car in front of us. Mother's posture was rigid. It looked like there was an imaginary string going up her neck and pulling her head straight up to the roof. Her slender fingers, wearing dainty white gloves, clenched the leather steering wheel in a death grip. I tipped my head against the window but kept a sideways glance at the landscape. At last, we crossed over the Bourne Bridge, leaving the Cape, and bound Northwest for Boston.

Once over the bridge, Mother shook her blue and gold paisley scarf free from her neck and flung it down on the arm rest as if she were throwing something rotten into the trash. She reached under the driver seat and pulled out a pack of cigarettes, the long brown skinny kind that she seemed to favor.

"Cigarette, Jack?" she said, shaking a few up and out of the pack as she tipped them in my direction. My head bounced off the window as she switched lanes.

"Excuse me?" I said.

"Oh, come on now, Jack. It's not like I don't know."

I shook one loose, then pushed in the car lighter. It popped out and I lit the cigarette off the flaming red light, passed it to mother, then took the one from her hand, and puffed away against the cherry coils until I got a good light.

"Thank you," I said, planting my foot on top of the dashboard and resting my hand on top of my knee.

I inhaled, exhaled, then chewed on my thumbnail all the while feeling self-conscious. Should I really be sitting here sharing a smoke with my own mother? I thought, angling myself toward the window so she couldn't catch a real glimpse of me.

I glimpsed over when she began rolling down her window, and watched as she threw her cigarette butt out on the road.

"I'd stuff it in the ashtray, but your father wouldn't *approve*," she said, waving her hand around in the air and rolling her eyes.

I flicked mine out the window, too.

Signs for Boston sprouted up along the highway the further we drove from the Cape. My heart thumped fast. We were getting closer to Cambridge.

"Harvard admissions, Jack. I can't believe the day is here," Mother said.

"Surreal," I said.

"My Jack, going on an interview at *Harvard University*." She reached over and tousled my hair. "I can't believe you're old enough for college, *college!* Why when I look at you I still see a little boy running around the house wearing a dish cloth as a cape!" She laughed, and so did I, but when I looked over she was dabbing tears away from her eyes. "I thought it would be nice if we had a late lunch afterward? We might walk around Cambridge a bit, see the sights. What do you say?" she said.

"I'd like that, Mother," I said. I was happy to spend time with her, and happier yet to prolong the return trip to Hyannis Port.

"The interview shouldn't last longer than an hour," I said. "What are you going to do while I'm in there?"

Mother pointed to the floor in the back seat. "I brought my camera. I thought I would stroll the campus. Look for some nice shots. I've been anxious to take new photos."

When Mother spoke about photography, her eyes sparkled, kind of like when the porch light at home beamed down on a fallen nighttime snow, and all you could see were the endless sparkling crystals. That's just what it was like. It was the light in the darkness.

Mother swerved along the busy streets of Cambridge with a sense of swagger, like she'd done this sort of thing many times. She squeezed the car between two others, gliding it in perfectly.

"Not bad!" I said in awe.

"Thank you!" she said, giving a short blast of the horn. Then she laughed, really laughed. A laugh of pure joy. Hearing Mother laugh like that was as refreshing as an ice cold glass of lemonade on a stifling hot day.

We stepped out of the car, but not before Mother rose up onto the edge of her seat and applied a fresh coat of red lipstick in the rearview mirror. I waited on the curb, hastily putting on my tie in the reflection of the car window, then bending down to look at my face in the side mirror, before licking my fingers and running them through my hair, trying to tame that cowlick that insisted on maddening me.

I fished some coins from out of my trouser pocket and dropped them into the meter. I'd been to Harvard a bunch of times before: football games, reunions, dropping off Thomas in August, picking him up again in May. And our house was somewhat of a shrine to the damn place, pictures mounted everywhere, coffee mugs filling the cabinets, sweatshirts and caps flooding the hall closet. But this visit was different because this visit was mine. Somehow that made it feel better than all of the other times.

"Jack," Mother said as we entered the main gate. She kept talking the whole time we walked along the sidewalks. I couldn't make out a single word she said; I was too busy studying everyone we passed. The guys had that same smug manner that Thomas had, and the girls seemed so bored, so goddamn bored. I had seen that type of boredom before and I despised it. It was that rich, entitled sense of boredom that lived in my neighborhood and showed up on our Hyannis Port vacations, the boredom that I loathed because it was such a sham. I knew it had to take effort to look so disinterested, and for the life of me, I couldn't imagine why anyone would drip so much energy into their own puddle of boredom.

Could I picture myself here among the Harvard folks? I wondered. I supposed I could in some ways. I knew how to play parts; I could easily play theirs. But did I *want* to play the part was altogether another question.

"Jack! I know you haven't heard one thing I've said, have you?" Mother stopped in her tracks and stuck her hands on her hips.

"Sorry," I said, scrunching my eyes in embarrassment. "Come on, Mother. Let's keep walking. I'll listen. I promise."

"What I was saying, Jack, is that when you go into your interview, don't mention a single thing about your father or your brother. Do you understand me? They are Harvard men, indeed, just like your grandfather was, but they are Harvard men for reasons much different from why you will be a Harvard man."

We picked up our pace as we walked toward the admissions building. Mother was talking fast like she wanted to make sure she said everything she had planned to say. This time I listened. I listened real hard.

"Your interview doesn't have to do with legacy, Jack. You've earned this more than any one of them has. So you make your interview about Jack Sullivan, no one else. Because you deserve this, Jack. *You* deserve Harvard and they deserve you. Now, I don't know what advice your father gave you this morning, but I feel it's important to give you my own."

I found this funny because Father hadn't given me any advice *except* to tell them that I was a Sullivan. Standing on the admission building's steps, Mother looked me straight in the eye and hushed her voice. She put both hands in mine. "Jack, when you walk into that interview room, I want you to walk into that room knowing that you are the most important person in there. Believe it, Jack, because you are. If you believe it, so will they. I love you so much, Jack. And I'm so, so proud of you. Now, I'll be waiting right here when you're through. Okay?"

"Okay," I said.

She squeezed my hands and kissed my cheek, then smoothed her hand down over my hair, and cupped my chin in her hand. "Go show them who Jack Sullivan is," she said. Then she put her handkerchief to her lips and I could tell she was fighting back more tears. She just kept staring at me, shaking her head, and smiling. She really loved me, my mother did.

A young man and his father pushed their way through the heavy wooden doors of the admission's building and there was nothing for me to do then but enter the building. I felt my breath fly out of me. It felt as if a vacuum had been pressed to my mouth and was sucking out all of the air. No matter how hard I tried to breathe, there was nothing there.

"Are you coming in?" the man said as held open the door.

I strained to get the words out. "Yes, sir. Thank you," I said.

"You're going to do great," Mother called after me, her hand half-raised to wave at me, her other hand resting against her cheek. I turned and waved back. She put her hand into a delicate fist and gave it a small upward shake. It made me smile watching Mother try her best to tell me to *go and get 'em.*

I sucked in all of the air I could and strode through the doors, my head held high, my shoulders squared, and my walk purposeful. I introduced myself to the secretary, an old-fashioned type who slid her black spectacles down her pointy nose and looked upward at me.

"You can wait in the library. It will be a few more minutes," she said, leading me down a gloomy, narrow hall.

The place was dead quiet. All I could hear were the scratchy sandpaper sounds that the secretary's stockings made each time she took a forward step. She led me into a sunny room. In the center of the floor lay a faded oriental rug. The walls were wood-paneled and boasted built in bookshelves loaded with hard cover books. I settled into a hunter green wingback chair, and stared out the tall windows. I could see Mother snapping pictures in the distance.

I looked around the room, took in a deep breath, then flattened my hair, wiped my brow, and pulled on my tie. I had the same feeling that consumed me whenever I'd waited in a doctor's reception area for the nurse to show up with her clipboard and call my name. I just wanted to get the damn thing over with.

I heard low murmurs coming from the room next door. I strained my ears real hard to pick up any words but I couldn't make anything out. The only thing I heard were the thank-yous and good-byes. Those parts were real loud, real clear. And then I heard the creak of the door, and the sound of shoes shuffling down the hall. *Shuffling*, I thought as I recalled Mother's advice about how to walk.

"Mr. Sullivan?" a tall man with a head full of silver hair said as he leaned past the doorway. He had a bit of that old Hollywood thing going for him, distinguished and all. His hair was slicked back, his teeth were near perfect, and his skin was real tan. I could picture him out sailing, not like the kind of boat my father might go on, but a real nice one, an old wooden schooner. The man was pure class.

"Yes, sir," I said, jumping up from my chair. I walked toward him, picking my feet up one at a time, careful not to slide them against the floor.

"Jack Sullivan, sir," I said, extending my hand.

"Jack Sullivan, I'm Michael Armstrong, Admission's Director. I've been looking forward to our meeting. We'll go right this way," he said, leading me into an immaculate office adorned with rowing oars hanging over a picture window, a brass lamp with a navy shade and thin gold piping, and a couple of Captain's chairs with the Harvard emblem scrolled across the back section.

Two men in suits stood side by side flashing indistinguishable smiles that showcased their gleaming teeth. How the hell does a guy get teeth as white as that? I thought. I prayed that I'd brushed mine well enough this morning as I opened my mouth to introduce myself to each of them. The first gentleman was a Professor, the second was an alum.

54

Mr. Armstrong took a seat behind his desk, also sitting in a Captain's chair. I noticed right away how smooth and shiny his desk was. How does a guy keep a desk so shiny? I thought, thinking about all the time I spent digging my pocketknife into my desk back home just to procrastinate from doing my schoolwork. But then, Mr. Armstrong didn't seem like the procrastinating type.

"Mr. Sullivan, it says here on your application that you are interested in history? Is that right?" Mr. Armstrong said, folding his hands, crossing one leg, and leaning back with a casual stance in his chair. My mind struggled to answer him, but somehow I couldn't help staring at his folded hands. Geez, the guy's nails were clean like he'd just washed them, and they were trimmed real short too. I cleared my throat and told myself to speak up already. Answer the man. As I did, I folded my hands also, but not before noticing the thin lines of dirt embedded in a few of my nails. Goddamn, I thought as I tucked my fingertips in to my palms and made loose fists.

"Yes sir, that's right. I have a passion for history," I said, even though I wasn't sure that I was much interested in history at all, not really. I just thought it would sound good on the application to at least be interested in something.

But before I knew it, the men in suits were firing off questions at me. And with one more deep breath, and the memory of Mother's advice, there I was answering them like I had known what the questions were going to be ahead of time. It was kind of like when you're reading a book and you get lost in the words and the next thing you know your mother's yelling upstairs for you to come down for dinner and you didn't even know that a whole hour had passed. That was what it was like, being swept away like that, and sure enough an hour had passed and the next thing I knew they were booming their thank-yous and good-byes, and there I was walking like a Navy cadet out of the place. I walked that way straight out of the building. I'm not saying I wasn't nervous as hell about the whole thing, I was, but it was like an out of body experience. It felt like some other guy had just slipped inside my body and started talking for me. And there those men were all smiling at me and at each other, and nodding, and acting all interested in everything I had to say. I kind of wished that other guy would pay me a visit more often, go ahead and do the speaking for me again like that, you know, like when Father yells at me to answer him about something and instead of answering him my mind just goes blank and I can't find a thing to say and he just goes on getting madder, or when one of my teachers asks me a question and I've been day-dreaming about hanging out with the guys on the weekend, throwing the ball around, and my mind goes empty except for the picture of me making a winning throw, and the pretty girl in the front row puts her head down to giggle, and there I sit with my mouth hanging open like a big dope trying to think of something, anything, so the teacher will just leave me alone. You know, at times like that.

Well, walking down the hall I felt that purpose Mother had told me about, and I began to think that maybe going to Harvard wouldn't be such a bad deal after all. Mr. Armstrong was chattering away about looking forward to receiving my Board scores, and he was sure I would fit right in on campus. But all I could think of was how thirsty I'd become, hell, after all of that talking, I was parched. It felt like all of the water had drained out of my body and pooled into my palms. I stuffed my clammy hands in my pants pocket, wiping them against the lining so Mr. Armstrong wouldn't cringe we shook good-bye.

"Thank you, sir," I said, as he led me to the same heavy doors I had entered through.

"Thank you, Jack. You have a notable background and I hope to make your acquaintance further next year," he said with a knowing nod.

I pushed through the door, bound down the stairs, and looked for Mother. I'm in, I thought. I'm going to be accepted at Harvard. The thought of it just about blew my mind. I jogged down the steps and looked around for Mother the way I did when I was little and found myself separated from her in the grocery store, running around and searching for her familiar face, hoping with every glance up the next aisle that she would be standing there. At Harvard, I ran up and down the pathways surrounding Harvard Yard, peered past each building, and then heaved a sigh of relief when in the middle of all things new, stood the face of home.

"Mother!" I said as she clicked a photo of a blue jay balancing on top of a small statue.

She twirled around. "Jack! Well?"

"I think I'm in. I think I've got it! And I think I might really like it here, Mother. I think I might if I try."

She grabbed me in a warm hug. "Oh, that's wonderful, Jack. Just wonderful! I'm so proud of you. Let's go have lunch. Time to celebrate!"

The walk felt light. My talking felt breathless and easy, and so sounded hers. Everything was wonderful in that moment, me sharing details of the interview from start to finish, her clinging to my every word. She stopped a few times to take more photos and seemed as proud of each snapshot as I'd felt coming out of my interview. She asked a young woman to take our picture and we sat down next to one another on an old bench. When we later approached the edge of campus that delivered us to the restaurants in Cambridge, I asked her, "Why don't you ever take your photos when we are with Father?"

"Oh, Jack," she said. "Your father thinks my photos are silly. To him, photography is just a waste of time."

"You know that's not true," I said.

"Of course, I do," she smiled. "But when you find your passion or when your passion finds you, you begin to realize how sacred of a thing it truly is. And, well, I guess we all have our admissions to make. If I was lucky enough to feel passionate about something in my life, *real passion*, then why on earth would I want to burn that flame around someone who just couldn't help himself but to stomp it out?"

"Thank you for taking your pictures around me," I said, linking my arm through hers as we headed to lunch.

She clutched the camera to her chest and rested her head on my shoulder as we continued to walk. "Ah, my darling boy. Thank you for being a spark in the fire."

MIDWAY

There is this thing that happens when people reach a midway point. A sense of urgency builds, the ride is almost over. People start asking questions: *Did we do everything we'd hoped?* They start making suggestions: *Let's pack in some more good times!* My Harvard interview marked the beginning of the third week of July and the midway point of our family vacation in Hyannis Port. Come August, there would be a new batch of hopefuls being served breakfast in the Honeysuckle dining room, and we would all be long gone.

I looked around at the families in the dining room that morning. I could sense that the feeling of new beginnings had passed. With that passing came melancholy eyes from some and jittery smiles from others, but for everyone there seemed a rush of all or nothing as we rounded the plate toward home at the Honeysuckle Inn.

I can't say that I felt the urgency I saw surfacing among the adults, but what I did find myself in was a comfortable groove. After each breakfast, I would make my way down to the beach. There was a section furthest away from the dune entrance where the other teenagers gathered. The younger kids hung around the outskirts. You could see from their longing eyes that they wanted so badly to abandon their parents' beach blankets, crawl out from underneath the massive umbrellas, and lounge around with us teenagers, but the invisible line was drawn in the sand and if you weren't at least fourteen, then you knew to keep on the family side.

I became friendly with the other young men staying at the Honeysuckle, and with each day, I became better friends with Isabelle Whitney, too. Izzy was always hanging around, and easy to be around at that. Some days, she'd be her kittenish self, and other times, she was as sarcastic as a salty sailor, but mostly, she was plain old fun.

Izzy and I paired up on most days. We'd do crosswords by the pool, eat cucumber and cream cheese sandwiches, and later on, try our hardest to sail the smallest damn thing that anyone ever dared called a sailboat. We laughed our asses off each time we took to the water, neither one of us knowing the rules of sailing, but having fun pretending all the same.

Izzy and I were like a traveling band. We came and went together, Izzy and I did. We'd stay out on the beach all day, riding the waves, telling stories with the others, smoking cigarettes and ashing into our makeshift ashtrays in the sand. When the other kids went back to the Inn, most often just before dusk, Izzy and I would pull our towels up over our shoulders, sink down low into the sand, and watch the beach empty out. The sparser the evening beach became, the more I think we felt free to be ourselves.

At long last, we'd drag ourselves up the Honeysuckle lawn and find the adults already dressed for cocktail hour. Someone was bound to yell at us not to track sand into the Inn. How ridiculous, I thought, as some old-timer would holler out to us, then wobble around on his feet and splash his drink all over the patio. Izzy and I would dunk our sandy feet into the pool when we thought nobody was looking. She would hold onto my arm and dip one foot in at a time and we would laugh all the while.

We'd dress for dinner and join the others in the main dining room, smiling at one another between the tables just to make it through the performance known as the family meal. In the evening, we would join a group for a bonfire and sneak a few beers. Or we might sit in on a game of cards in the parlor. The events changed each night, though the one thing that remained the same was our night's end. Izzy and I had made a habit of sneaking into one another's rooms after our parents went back downstairs for their nightcaps. I loved that part of our day the best, when we would reacquaint with one another free from the guise of our families and the Honeysuckle way. Just like those few times we'd gone skinny dipping, we'd turn away from the other to undress and drop our clothes in a pile on the ground, then dive under without ever stealing a glance of one another. In the bed, nothing in the world felt better than the crisp cotton sheets against my bare sun soaked skin, nothing except for Izzy's arm grazing mine when she flipped her pillow over, and that small spark that I felt fly through me whenever her skin glided against mine.

"I love the cold side of the pillow, don't you, Jack?" she'd say.

"Sure do, Iz." I'd say.

"What else do you love, Jack?"

And so our nights went. We were both on a full speed search for the answers to our own lives, so our friendship made sense. There was an endless comfort that we found in one another's certainties and uncertainties.

"Night, Jack," she'd yawn.

"Night, Iz," I'd say, and we'd roll away from one another, facing the outside.

By morning, Izzy would be gone before anyone else might get up and see her sneaking down the hall. Of course, I knew that when I woke she'd be gone, but that never stopped me from reaching out for her. A heap of sheets was all that awaited me. It was a bittersweet start to my day because as soon as I'd wake I'd find myself missing her. And let me tell you, it isn't easy missing someone that was never yours.

*****

"Going down to the beach, Jack?" Izzy said as we left the dining room after breakfast.

"Hey, Iz, what do you say to some exploring? I'm sure there's more to the Cape than what's going on around here," I said.

She twirled her ponytail with her index finger. "What do you have in mind?"

"I don't know, maybe hitch a ride somewhere."

"Jack!"

"C'mon, Iz! It'll be fun. I'm going up to get some money from my drawer. I'll meet you outside in ten minutes."

Izzy stood staring at me with a tight smile.

"It'll be fun. I swear to it!" I said, taking the stairs two at a time.

"Oh, all right," she said. "But don't breathe a word of this to anyone, Jack. My father would have a fit if he found out I left the Honeysuckle."

"One more reason why we should do it!" I reached the top of the stairs and leaned over. Izzy put her finger in her mouth and chewed it like she wasn't too sold on my idea.

"Iz?" I said, hanging over the banister. "I promise not to tell."

"Ok," she said, her shoulders relaxing and a smile spreading across her face. "I'll meet you outside then."

"And Iz?'

"Yes, Jack?"

"I promise you are going to have real fun."

Izzy was sitting on the front steps, her knees pulled right up underneath her chin. I tugged her ponytail and ran past her. "C'mon, c'mon!" I said. She ran to keep up with me, but I didn't stop until we'd rounded the mailbox and were clear out of sight. I slowed down and waited for her. We doubled over laughing to catch our breath.

"I sure hope we aren't running to wherever it is we're going," she said.

"No, no. Just hauled out of there so we wouldn't get caught. C'mon let's walk down this way, it should take us to the main road." We slowed down. Our breathing steadied. The road was still.

"So where do you want to go today, Iz?"

"Me? Heavens, I don't know!"

"It's your adventure, too. Isn't it?"

"Well, I've always wanted to go to Provincetown. Any idea where that is?" she laughed.

"Provincetown? Yeah, last point on the Cape. I'm sure we can find someone headed that way."

"You're sure this is such a good idea?" she said, nibbling on that finger of hers like she was a mouse.

"Sure, Iz. People hitch all the time," I said, walking backward with my thumb out in the air. "Plus, I'm here, aren't I? I'll take care of you."

After about half-dozen cars, a rusty station wagon pulled over and some quiet college-aged kid rolled down his window about half an inch.

"Any chance you're headed to Provincetown?" I said.

"Yes. Hop in," the driver said.

Izzy and I piled in, then gripped one another's hands against the back seat as the station wagon sped off down the road. I tried striking up a conversation with the fella driving. He just stared at me through the rearview mirror, staring through those thick coke bottle glasses of his. Izzy and I barely spoke a word the whole way there. I think both of us were too busy covering our noses. The car resembled something closer to Thomas' sock drawer. She looked up at me with raised eyebrows. I smiled and nodded, though this wasn't quite the idea I had when I dreamt up my first hitchhiking ride.

The kid dropped us off a half-mile from Provincetown and we laughed the whole walk to Main Street, belly laughs over this stranger who'd been driving us, how he kept the windows rolled closed, and blew his nose into an old shirt, and how he didn't mutter a word to us the entire time.

"I've never been happier than when he put on the brakes!" Izzy said.

"Sorry Iz, that's not quite the ride I'd expected," I said, wiping my brow.

Izzy laughed and laughed. "Oh, sometimes those are the best rides, aren't they Jack? The unexpected ones?" We stopped for a moment and stared at one another. It was kind of intense, the way we stared like that.

"Yeah, Iz. I suppose those are the best rides."

Izzy and I strolled down Main Street. Provincetown. Hell, I'd never been to anyplace like it. Everyone was smiling and laughing and having a good time. The shops were full of all this cool art, really wild pictures, wild colors and shapes. The art wasn't anything like I'd ever seen before. People were dressed real artsy, too. I felt a little out of place, like I was too preppy or something, even though, believe me, I'm the first one to hate being raised a prep. The guys in Provincetown walked around shirtless, wearing faded, ripped jeans and brown leather sandals. The girls wore these mismatched patterned dresses and went barefoot with jewelry dangling around their ankles and little rings on their toes. Izzy and I soaked it all in. We loved every minute of it.

At lunch, we stopped at a clam shack. We sat on a bench, our food on oily paper plates in between us, and we gorged ourselves on fried clam strips, French fries, and pop. If Ms. Gardenia could see us now, we laughed, wiping our greasy hands against our shorts, and licking our salty lips.   After lunch, we headed for the beach, but not before buying weed off some old-timer sitting at the end of the pier.

"You sure you want to do this?" I asked Iz, because I wasn't too sure if I really wanted to. I guess I just thought it might be kind of cool if we did. I half-hoped she'd say no, to get me out of the mess of asking in the first place, but no, she said yes, and there I was chatting up this guy who was strumming a guitar and singing about a moonbeam over the water. Before I knew it, Izzy and I were sitting on the rocks and listening to him sing about those moonbeams. Hell, I thought I might even be riding one. Izzy and I were just stoned out of our minds.

When we left to walk down the beach, I found myself in that blurry place in my head where my mind posts a *do not enter* sign and refuses to entertain any of the thoughts that always seem to be banging around up there. Izzy just giggled. She giggled in a way so sweet that I couldn't help myself but to reach out for her and sling my arm over her shoulder. We walked ourselves along the beach, bumping into each other with every few steps.

I knew our time away from the Honeysuckle was short. Our folks would be looking for us back at the Inn anytime now. I spotted a sandy trail through the dunes that carried us to the beach road. I stuck out my thumb. In minutes, we'd hitched a ride back to Hyannis Port from a Portuguese grandmother who was heading that way. I figure she was a grandmother because she was kind of old, and her tan skin had deep wrinkles, and there were pictures of herself with children eating cake and smiling taped across her dashboard. She noticed the camera hanging down around my neck, actually one of Mother's old ones, and she smiled and asked if we'd like our photo taken together. Sure, we said. Why not. And so, smooshed in the tiny backseat, with our arms slung over one another's shoulders, we smiled and laughed as the Portuguese grandmother snapped a photo of us and then turned to drive on.

Izzy hummed a folk song and rested her head on my shoulder. I turned my head and looked out the window on Izzy's side, the seaside. All the windows were rolled down halfway when we'd hopped in and now with the car picking up speed as we headed along the coast, the smell of salt water whipped straight through the car, circling around us and engulfing our senses before blowing out the window on the other side. I looked over at the shore and watched the waves crashing about, the whitecaps on the tips, the gulls circling for food and swooping down to the beach. The breeze sure had picked up.

I watched Isabelle's face through the rearview mirror. She looked so peaceful, Isabelle did. Her eyes were closed. A soft smile crossed her pink lips. Her cheeks were peachy looking with a few freckles crossing the bridge of her nose. The sun filtered through the window, radiating off of her golden, freckled shoulders. I closed my eyes too, and inhaled that sweet, musky sweat that I remembered of her after our first tennis match.

Izzy laid her hand on mine and made little circles along my knuckles with her fingertips. Her touch was so light it felt like she was holding a feather in her hand. I opened my eyes and watched in the mirror as she wiggled her shoulders, nestling herself into the crook of my neck. The Portuguese grandmother glanced back at us, the tired gaze of her brown eyes lifting. Izzy's soft purrs escaped until she settled her head. She released a long, satisfied hum after she'd found her perfect spot.

"Oh, Jack," she said, smiling lightly.

Izzy's fingers had come to a rest, but she kept her hand on top of mine. I linked my fingers through hers, leaned my ahead back against the head rest, and shut my eyes. She tilted her body further into mine, and our heads met at one another's temples. I breathed in deep, then closed my eyes. I could feel a tiny pulse and kind of made me feel choked up for a moment; it reminded me of the absolute intensity of life that lives in the slightest of private moments. The sounds and scents of the Atlantic continued to surge through the car. In between each whoosh of wind were the sounds of Izzy's little breaths. Hearing those breaths made me feel all filled up inside, and all I could do was smile because Izzy felt like home.

Back at the Inn, Izzy headed straight to her room without eating, said she needed a nap. I grabbed some food by the pool and decided to stick it out with the others for a while. I loaded my plate up with two burgers, macaroni salad, and a pile of bread and butter pickles. I made my way back to my room as soon as I'd finished my meal.

The sun had made me feel groggy and mere minutes after crawling in between my sheets, I began to doze. It was the click of the door that woke me. My fear of old lady Gardenia sneaking into my room was long gone. I didn't even open my eyes. Of course it was Isabelle. I heard her slipping out of her robe, then the heavy thud of the terry cotton upon the hardwood floor. I heard the creaking of the wooden planks as she tip-toed on the balls of her feet around the foot of the bed. I waited for her to crawl in beside me, nuzzle her chin into my pillow and let out her soft purrs, but the wait seemed long.

I opened my eyes to see her stark naked, soft and round in all the ways I'd imagined. Her body shone in the moonlight. She stood by the window and stared out to sea, then turned to find me gawking at her. I imagine I had a stupid look on my face because she criss-crossed her arms in front of her chest and did a little trot over to the bed as if she was embarrassed that I had seen so much of her. She must have expected I'd been fast asleep.

Everything seemed strange at once. We had lain naked next to one another the whole week now. We'd felt the heat from one another bodies against our skin, but we'd never stopped and taken a real look at each other. Izzy lay flat on her back. She grasped the covers up underneath her chin and took in sharp little breaths.

I couldn't look at her. I rolled onto my side, afraid of her seeing my face, me the one who had caught too much sight of her. And now that I had seen her, seen all of her, I couldn't help but want all of her too. And now that I wanted all of her, the only thing I could think to do was ignore her, lest she think that I wanted her and get uncomfortable, lest I ruin everything that we had created as friends.

"What are you thinking, Jack?" she said.

"Nothing really," I said through a fake yawn.

"Jack?" she said. The way she said my name was so vulnerable. It was the type of vulnerability in a girl that makes you want to cradle her and never let go until she's an old woman and you've made a long life together somewhere far away in a cluttered old farm house with rooms full of memories. You know the kind of memories I mean, like dragging the first snowy Christmas tree through the door, or her rounded belly with the third or fourth child, or the way she makes slow figure eights with a wooden spoon as she stirs a tall glass pitcher of lemonade, or the shadows of her curves underneath a white cotton nightgown as she stands by an open window on a sweltering summer night.

Some time passed. "Jack? Are you awake?" she said.

I fought to answer her. I was dying to talk to her, dying to touch her. But I kept my mouth shut. I pressed my lips so hard together that I was sure they'd be bruised by the morning.

I woke in the middle of the night plagued with guilt. My mouth was dry. My heart pounded. I opened my eyes and stared straight ahead at the place where I had seen her the night before. I reached down underneath the covers to take hold of her hand. I was sorry for ignoring her the night before. I was sorry if I'd made her feel bad. But the space next to me was nothing but a pile of sheets. Midway through, and Isabelle Whitney was gone.

I didn't see Isabelle at the beach the next day, nor the one after that. I knew I would see her at the Honeysuckle dinner party that weekend. It was the biggest party of the summer, held in celebration of the July guests. There'd be appetizers, cocktails, a soul band, even fireworks to end the night. She just had to be there.

LAST DANCE

I closed the door of my room, adjusted my tie, shook loose my shoulders, and walked down the hall, slicking my hair back with my hand and nodding as I passed the young couple staying in the room next to me. It was kind of hard to look either of them in the eye, what with the way their bed had squeaked away every night since I'd arrived here.

My eyes drifted to the sight of Ms. Gardenia standing at the platform landing of the staircase. Her lips were painted a fierce shade of red, her skin had thick white powder set onto it and made her face look like a giant pancake. She greeted each guest who made their way downstairs. Beyond Ms. Gardenia, my eyes settled on the white glove resting on the stairwell, the blonde ponytail pulled high above the swanlike bend of the neck, the wisps of baby hair at the nape, and the pale blue evening dress with the single white ribbon wrapped around the waist. Isabelle Whitney. She was there.

I wished that I could have gone and bumped up alongside her like I would have done earlier in the week. You know, that I could have tossed my arm around her shoulder, pecked her cheek in a friendly way, then strolled inside the parlor with her, breaking into a partnered dance at the first sound of the brass horns. But at first glimpse of me, Isabelle looked down at her hands and pulled at the fingertips of her dainty gloves.

"Good evening, Isabelle," I said.

"Jack," she said.

"Yes?" I said.

"Oh, I wasn't asking you a question, Jack," she said as her face flushed with berry red splotches.

"I'm real sorry, Isabelle."

Her chest rose high as she drew in a deep breath. I could see she was trying to control the release as she exhaled through her nostrils.

"Don't be silly, Jack. Honest mistake. I could have very well been asking you a question."

67

My throat tightened. More people were coming down the stairs.

"I'm sorry for the other night, I mean," I said, though I felt like I could never quite explain what I truly meant.

Thomas caught sight of us. "Save me the first dance, won't you, Isabelle?" he said in his garish voice.

"I'll have to check my dance card, Thomas," she said, brushing her gaze against the floor before batting her lashes and lifting her eyes lightly up to meet mine as Thomas walked away.

"May I have the first dance, Isabelle?" I said, resting my hand on hers.

"I had hoped so, Jack," she said.

We walked like strangers into the dining room, the air between us thick.

Goddamit, I thought. Why the hell did I have to mess everything up the last time she was in my room. Now everything felt awkward between us, and to be honest, I was dreading dancing with her at all.

"I see my mother and father. I'll find you when the band plays," I said.

"Ok, Jack," she said and stole away to a group of girls hovering by the punch bowl.

It wasn't so much that I wanted to say hello to my mother and father as it was I wanted to distance myself from the discomfort that I had created between Isabelle and myself.

"Why Jack, don't you look handsome," Mother said, kissing my cheek and smoothing down my cowlick.

"Cleaned up well for the festivities, son," Father said, slapping my back so hard I wondered what the hell was the matter with him.

I rubbed Mother's lipstick smudge off my cheek, then returned a hard slap to my father's back, wiping my hand against his suit at the same time. It was the little paybacks I enjoyed, when I could fit them in, anyhow. Father, the ignorant fool, seemed to like the playful banter. He was probably proud I was developing into a regular old smart ass like he and Thomas. Mother sipped her cocktail and waved her index finger back and forth, though I could see the smile on her lips behind the upward tipped glass.

I leaned back and looked down the corridor leading to the kitchen. I saw Maybelle heaving all of her weight into a large cart crammed full with silver platters of hors d'oeuvres.

"Excuse me," I said to my parents as I hurried toward the door.

"Maybelle? Here Maybelle, let me help you with that," I said as she patted beads of sweat off her forehead with a tissue, took in a deep breath, and smoothed out her apron.

"I'd be much obliged, Jack. Thank you," she said. "Cart's so full it's hard to get it through the doorway!"

"You just tell me where," I said, pushing it through the crowd. Old man Parker, one of Father's golf buddies, cleared his throat, then burned his eyes into me as I wheeled past him. I couldn't help but ask God to send him straight to hell, but knowing God wasn't likely to answer me, I shifted the cart wheels a hair too close to his shoe.

"Ouch!" he said, jumping back and sputtering under his breath like a busted old car engine.

"Mr. Parker, excuse me, sir," I said.

He kept on sputtering, and I kept on smiling as I followed Maybelle to an empty space next to the fireplace. Ah, the fireplace, the one spot that I loved the most. It crackled and sent red hot embers soaring about like miniature firecrackers. It glowed orange like a harvest moon. It was beautiful.

I parked the cart and smiled at Maybelle, then sat down in the nearest chair and snatched a few bacon wrapped scallops before the other scavengers ate them all up. I leaned forward and rested my elbows on my knees. I cocked my head and stared into the fiery pit. I let my mind go blank until I heard the tip-tap of high heels and saw the baby blue satin shoes in front of me. I looked up to see Isabelle with her arms crossed in front of her matching dress. Her head was tilted and she stared off to the side of me, twirling her ponytail around her finger. She stuck her right hip out, and bent her left foot at the

69

ankle. When I looked at her long enough, she turned and stared hard into the fire. I reached out for her hand, untangled her fingers, and stood up beside her.

"The band looks like it's getting ready to play," I said.

"I see that," she said, biting the inside of her cheek. I watched the reflection of the fireplace flames dance in her eyes.

"May I still have that first dance, Isabelle?"

She curled her chin down to her neck and whispered, "Yes."

We walked onto the dance floor and I was never happier then when a slow, bluesy tune floated out of the instrument horns. We danced real close. She looked over my shoulder, and I was grateful that I didn't have to look her in the eyes, grateful that we didn't have to search out one another's faces and try to figure out what the other one might be thinking.

Isabelle was still the girl that felt like home, the only girl whose friendship had immediately matched that of any fella I'd known, but seeing her by the window that night flicked a switch in my brain. It was the same switch that had flicked on that afternoon at the tennis court, the switch that had gone off after I'd taken care of her on that morning she'd lain helpless in the dunes. But now the switch was back on again, and I feared I would never be able to treat her like plain old Izzy. How quickly she returned to being Isabelle Whitney.

Isabelle rested her hand on my shoulder and laid her cheek against it. I couldn't see her face, but I felt her mulling over something.

"Jack?" she said.

"Yeah, Isabelle?" I said.

"Jack are you mad at me about something? Did I do something wrong?"

I pulled back and looked at her, feeling terrible that she felt at fault about anything.

"Of course not, Isabelle. No, no. You didn't do anything wrong. That's why I said I was sorry earlier on by the stairs. There's not one thing you did wrong." I pushed a strand of her hair out of her eyes and tucked it behind her ear.

She placed her hand on my shoulder and rested her chin against it. She sighed. "Do you feel like dancing, Jack?" she said.

"Naw, not really," I said. Her body froze. "But I want to stay with you, Isabelle. I do. It's not that I don't want to be with you. I'm just not in the mood to dance around is all."

"Me neither," she said, looking over her shoulder, then spinning back to look at me with a sparkle in her eye. "Jack, Marcia Foss spiked the punch bowl. Should we have a drink?"

"That sounds great, Izzy," I said. She shone as I called her that. Funny how things just slipped right back into place between us. Guess there was nothing for me to get so nervous about after all.

By the punch bowl, I filled two crystal goblets sky high with pink juice. We gulped the first round then refilled our glasses before strolling around the parlor. She slid her arm through mine. Ah, Izzy.

We enjoyed commenting on our parents and the company they kept. The men looked dapper, the women ostentatious. "They're like plastic clones of one another, aren't they?" Isabelle said as we walked by one couple after another. The men all spoke in the same pitched voice, the women all laughed at exactly the same time.

The parlor room looked like a heavy fog had rolled in as cigarette smoke filled the air. The hors d'oeuvres stations were soon empty, a fact that didn't seem to matter much to the inebriated folks who grabbed the hands of anyone around them. They pulled one another out onto the dance floor and shook their bodies to the sounds that rocked the Honeysuckle Inn in ways that surprised me. Old lady Gardenia slithered like a snake around some poor soul, and my stomach convulsed at the sight. She wore a slinky black number and kept pulling on the ends of a gray feather boa that she had draped around her neck. Maybelle came in to retrieve the empty food platters and I laughed to see her hips shimmy and shake as she wheeled the cart back into the kitchen.

After our third walk around the dance floor, and our third stop at the punch bowl, the room seemed to be tilting like a slanted picture frame on a wall. The music blared.

71

The adults blurred together, a sea of golden skinned bodies in evening wear. Izzy and I stumbled against one another with every other step until she yanked my arm out toward the dance floor, holding on to my shoulders and laughing and rocking backward on her high heels.

I tripped over my own feet, then toppled straight onto Izzy before she pushed me upward, grabbed both of my hands and broke into a makeshift jive. I had never felt as alive as I had in that moment. Our faces were flushed, our laughter loud, and our feet fast. For the first time since arriving at the Honeysuckle, I wasn't taking notice of everyone around me. It felt like the tables had turned, that the others were noticing me now, and that Izzy and I were at the center. Quite frankly, I felt like I was on top of the world.

The song ended in a bang and Izzy and I clutched one another. Izzy was giddy, leaning over and clapping her hands and laughing. I was yelping along with the blaring sounds of the band. With our arms wrapped tight around one another's backs, we swerved off the dance floor, laughing our asses off.

"Nice moves, son," Father yelled as he hustled by us, shuffling his feet backward and waving his thumbs in the air. He made his way onto the dance floor to join a raucous group of men and women. I laughed, happy that the old man was enjoying himself.

Mother stood like a statue by the side of her table. Her arms were crossed over her waist. The only movement was in her wrist when she brought the thin brown cigarette up to her mouth and then down again.

"Isabelle, I think I'll ask my mother to dance," I said.

"Thatta boy, Jack!" Mr. Whitney blurted out as he came toward us, taking Isabelle by the hand and leading her away for a dance. Isabelle giggled all the while, then called out, "Meet me back by the fireplace!"

"Sure thing!" I said, heading over to Mother's side.

"May I have this dance, Mother?" I said, extending my hand.

"Oh, Jack, I don't know," she said, fumbling the end of the cigarette between her thumb and forefinger. "Oh, what the hell! Why not!" She leaned over and stubbed the cigarette out in the dumbwaiter.

"C'mon!" I said, pulling her out on the dance floor before the song had a chance to end. I twirled her around and she laughed and laughed. She was a pretty good dancer, my mother was. Twirling around with her like that brought me back to our kitchen in Ithaca when Thomas and I were little kids. Mother would play music on the small black radio by the kitchen window once we'd finished our breakfast and Father had left for work. We'd sit slurping the leftover milk from our cereal bowls, watching her wash the dishes, and all of a sudden she'd turn around with a glorious smile and say, "Let's have a dance, boys!" And away we would go. Thomas would run up to plant his little feet on top of hers as I scooted up her leg until she had me on her hip. The three of us would dance and spin. Thomas would put his hand up on my chubby leg, and I'd put my little sausage fingers on Mother's shoulder. We'd both hold on tight while she spun us around, dancing and laughing and singing the sweetest sounds I'd ever heard. The morning sun would peek in through the lemon print curtains above the kitchen sink window, and I'd close my eyes and soak in its glow, savoring the vibration of Mother's voice singing against my cheek, and the security of Thomas's hand on my leg.

My memory broke as Mother clapped at the end of the song. I wiped my eye, and hugged her tight. "Thanks, for the dance," I said, when in my heart I was thanking her for a childhood of dances, I just didn't how to say all that.

"Thank you, Jack!" she said. "That was real fun."

Father came up behind her as the singer announced, "Time to slow things down around here." The band cooed while couples swayed. I noticed then just how graceful Mother was, and how clumsy Father was, tripping all over her in his drunken stupor, roaring with laughter as he whipped her around in circles. What a buffoon, I thought, shaking my head.

I caught sight of Isabelle waiting by the fireplace and my insides glowed at the thought of her loyalty to me. I couldn't get over to her fast enough.

"Izzy!" I winked, the spiked punch having set in.

Tiny hiccups gurgled out of her throat. I imagined little soap bubbles floating from her mouth each time she made a sound. I slunk down in the nearest seat and pulled her down onto my lap, my hand falling loosely upon her knee. Any other time I would have obeyed the behavior codes around the Honeysuckle, but one look around the room and anyone could tell that most folks were too blasted to notice us kids anyway.

"Isabelle Whitney, you turned this summer into something quite spectacular," I said.

"Why, thank you, Jack Sullivan," she said, speaking with a playful smile through pursed lips. She pressed her forehead against mine. "Look at all these half-empty glasses," she said, eyeing the dozen or so mixed drinks abandoned on the tables over the course of the night. "Shall we?" She picked up a clear beverage with a twisted lemon rind floating around the top.

"Absolutely," I said, sampling a tall glass of beer two thirds full, determined to get drunk for no reason at all. I'd had a few beers before, but never really been smashed. And with Izzy as my partner in crime, the offer seemed too hard to refuse. She and I babbled our way through our alcohol sampling until we were roaring with laughter and nearly tipping out of our chairs.

"Pardon me, Jack. I need to use the ladies' room," she said. She broke into fits of laughter as she banged the chair around, trying to move it away from the table. She stumbled away, tumbling over her feet and colliding into the neighboring table before zigzagging across the floor and heading out the door.

I laughed to myself at the absurdity of getting drunk off of other people's floaters, then let my eyes zone in on a green glass ashtray at the far end of the table. I decided it was high time that I smoked a cigarette with a little more pride than I'd done before. I was tired of sneaking smokes here and there and gargling with mouthwash so I wouldn't get caught. To hell with it, I thought, and shook one loose from a crammed soft pack abandoned in the middle of the table. I turned back toward the fire, lit the cigarette and flicked the end, spewing ashes everywhere and not giving a damn about the mess I was leaving behind. I leaned back, crossed one leg over my knee, and shook my head as I sank my front teeth down into the filter. What a night, I thought.

"Young man," Ms. Gardenia said, tugging on my ear. "Young man, you put that out right now. You are far too young to be smoking. You'll paint a bad image for the Inn."

"Yes, Ma'am," I said as I puffed away. I stood up, continued smoking, then flashed my craziest smile at her as I walked backward out of the room.

"Why, I *never*," she said. I couldn't hear the rest of her griping because her sounds had begun to blend together like everything else that night.

I turned around and concentrated on placing one foot in front of the other until I was well out of the room. I waited in the foyer near the hall bathroom for Isabelle. Drinking so much had left me barely able to stand when it came time. I leaned back against the foyer wall and slumped down while trying to keep myself propped up. Izzy staggered out of the bathroom and walked straight by me.

"Izzy! *Psst!* Izzy!" I said.

"Jack! What are you doing on the floor!" she laughed, then slid down beside me, landing with a plunk. Her head flopped on my shoulder and she swayed side to side humming her folk songs. With her head resting on my shoulder like that, I felt like we were right in the car of the Portuguese grandmother driving us back from Provincetown. Ah, Izzy.

Isabelle sprang up on her knees, scrambled to her feet, and braced my shoulders with both of her hands. "Jack! I've just remembered. Fireworks!" she said, sparkles dancing wildly in her eyes.

"Fireworks?" I said, scratching my head and yanking my tie loose.

"Yes, Jack. Fireworks! Ms. Gardenia said there would be fireworks on the beach tonight."

On cue, the parlor doors swung open and hordes of drunken folks rushed past us chattering: "Fireworks! On the beach! Ten minutes! Let's go!"

"C'mon, Jack!" Isabelle said, scurrying onto her feet and making her best attempt at yanking me up from the floor.

"Why not," I said.

We fell into the scuttle, then broke free from the pack when we hit the dunes. We jetted off onto the beaten trail the teenagers had claimed, then spilled out onto a stretch of beach ablaze with a bonfire and littered with empty cans of beer.

I looked down the beach and saw Mother already sitting with a circle of women on a blanket, laughing and pouring red wine from a bottle. Thomas was standing with a group of guys, making loud sounds, "Bam! Pop! Whish!" every time a firework flew off the beach and over the water. The guys around him burst into laughter as if they'd never heard anything so original.

"C'mere, Iz" I said, slurring my words as I pulled her down beside me. We lay back on the sand and stared up at the glimmering sparks of yellow, blue, red, and green that erupted across the sky. Like dripping colors from the rainbow, they splattered down into the water until they fizzled out to black.

I closed my eyes. As a kid, the sounds of the mini-explosions had scared the hell out of me. Yet lying there on the beach with Izzy in the crook of my arm, I found the sounds so peaceful that I could have drifted asleep.

"Jack," she whispered.

"Yeah, Iz," I said.

"Jack, Daddy has some marijuana hidden upstairs in his drawer. I overheard him telling one of the other men about it last night. He does that sort of thing from time to time, you know."

"No, I didn't know."

"Do you want to smoke some, Jack? We could sneak up to his room while everyone's down on the beach, then come back here later tonight to smoke it. Do you want to, Jack?"

I pecked the top of her head then rose up from the sand. "Let's go quick, before anybody sees us," I said.

76

We crouched down real low and snuck up to the great lawn of the Inn. I searched for any sign of movement in the parlor windows. Long shadows of people holding instruments scaled the wall. I took a breath, grateful it was just the guys in the band. We snuck through the front door, looking over to see the band packing their instruments into their cases. One of the guys was leaning back against a wall and gulping down a bottle of beer. Another guy was chatting up Maybelle in the corner. She seemed to be sweet on him by the curvy smile that crossed her lips. One of them looked over at us as the wood creaked beneath our feet. We hung our heads down low and picked up the pace. I reached my hand back for Isabelle's and pulled her along with me. The last thing we needed was to be found out while trying to steal marijuana from her father's drawer.

"We made it," I said, stopping on the stair landing to catch my breath. "Which one is your parents' room?"

"Sixth room on the right," she said. "Here, I'll lead the way. They usually leave the door unlocked. Let's hope they did tonight." She tiptoed down the hall, then looked back at me with an impish smile. It was hard not to adore her.

Izzy put her finger to her lips and snuck on, waving me after her. Beside each door were mounted lights. The corridor of blaring beams sobered me. I couldn't wait to be back down on the sand, smoking with her, gazing out at the stars and letting the ocean waves drown out everything around us.

She sped up her pace and I tried to keep up with her. When I passed my room, I noticed a stream of light sliding out from beneath the door. That's strange, I thought, remembering that I'd turned off the lamp next to my bed and given the door a hearty slam before leaving my room for the dinner party.

"Hey, Iz," I murmured. "I'll meet you back at the stairs. I gotta turn off my light."

"Ok," she said, holding up crossed fingers before turning her parents' door and slipping inside.

Anxious to join her, I rushed inside my room to turn out the light. As I turned the switch off an eerie vision of old lady Gardenia floated around inside my head. I felt for the wall as I hurried out of the dark room. A sliver of light peeked out from beneath the bathroom door and onto the carpet. Shit, I thought, as I grasped the doorknob and turned to realize that I must have left the bathroom light on as well. In the pitch black, my drunkenness seemed to resurface. I took a few quick stumbles, then crashed against the bathroom door. When it flung open, I fought to catch my balance, feeling like I had just stepped off of a roller coaster.

My eyes adjusted to the light when I saw a woman's face staring at me in shocked horror. Splayed over the middle-aged female with the messy black bouffant, and one missing gold earring, was my father. His trousers harnessed his feet at the ankles, his pale flat ass stared me straight in the face, thrusting and pumping in between the legs of the two bit whore who, all summer long, had posed as one of the many perfect Honeysuckle housewives.

Father groaned out like a dying animal, collapsing down on her body and smashing his mouth against her silver dollar nipples with loud, wet smacks. She looked like she'd seen a ghost, staring at me with that crooked look on her face. Her face looked like it was pressed up flat against a window. Her eyes were contorted. Her painted lips took on the shape of a square. She raised her hand to point at me but I turned and ran, not wanting to meet the eyes of the old bastard who called himself my father.

I found that when I ran, I didn't stumble. I flew like a fierce wind was tackling my backside and my legs couldn't slow down even if they wanted to. I sprinted by Izzy who was waiting with a victorious smile at the bottom of the stairs.

"Jack?" she said. "Jack!"

I couldn't stop. I wanted to, but I couldn't. I ran straight out of the Honeysuckle and high-tailed it down the driveway.

"Jack!" she called, and breathless, I knew that she was running after me.

"Goddamit!" I slurred. How I wanted to run until I couldn't stop. Run until I had exhausted myself. Run until I came to the beach and had nowhere to escape but straight into the ocean water. Run and run and run until the current trapped my legs, until I fought for one last breath, until I was gone. But then a damn rut snuck up underneath my foot and I flew into a dip in the road. I stood up and scrambled for rocks, heaving them in the direction of where I wanted to go. I crawled off to the side, the calls of Izzy echoing in my ear. I gagged and spit and spewed out coarse grains of sand from my mouth. I dug it out of my ears. Wiped it from my eyes. I was a fucking mess. I leaned over into the bushes, hurling the mix of drinks until my stomach heaved, churning and twisting itself dry like a wet towel.

Izzy fell down on her knees on the ground beside me. She stroked the back of my neck. She pulled my handkerchief out of my pocket, spit into it, then rubbed the dirt off my face.

"What happened?" she hushed.

"Fuck him!" I said.

"Who, Jack?"

"Fuck the world!"

"Why, Jack?"

"Why? *Why?* Fuck 'em all, Isabelle, because they don't give a royal fuck about us. My father, *my father*, wants me to be a dick, a regular old cock, and now I know why. Do you want to know why, Isabelle? Do you *really* want to know why?"

"Why, Jack?"

"Because the more of an asshole I become, the more of a man he'll think that he is. He won't see himself as too bad in the mirror if the men around him look like shit, too. And they do, Iz. You know they do, too. All of 'em. They're fucking wafting in their own shit. Don't you think it's odd the way they all went to the same fucking schools? Or how they all vacation in the same fucking places? What the *fuck* is that all about? I'll tell you what it's about, Iz," I said, spitting sand out of my mouth.

"What's it about, Jack?"

"Their fucking fearful fucks, Isabelle. Their fucking ego mad. Talking to one another is like jerking their own chains in public. Feels pretty good to 'em. Then they go on and jerk one another off every time they talk about their *good ol' days*. And don't even get me started on their kids. You've got those young assholes out there *finding themselves* on some overpriced tour of Europe or something. Who the fuck finds themselves at sixteen-years old on a *guided* European tour? I know I didn't. Did you, Iz? Did you?"

"No, Jack."

"Of course not. But they'd like us to believe that alright. Well, I don't know about you, but I never found myself while hunkered down at some resort with a bunch of other preppies. But I'll tell you where I am finding myself."

"Where's that, Jack?"

"I'm finding myself right here, Isabelle. Right here with my pathetic, middle-aged father fucking some dirty old whore on my bathroom floor. That's where I'm finding myself. I'm finding myself thinking of my mother, my poor, sweet mother, who has to put up with absolute bullshit. Now that's finding yourself, Iz."

"I see, Jack."

I looked up at Isabelle. She gave subtle nods as she listened to my vulgar rant.

"I'm so angry, Iz," I said, feeling the fury rising up through my body until it purged itself from my mouth and pierced the static night air. I screamed so loud my body quavered. I wanted to hit something, anything, so I dropped onto all fours and attacked the earth beneath me. I sat up and screamed louder this time, a primal scream from the pits of my stomach, a scream so raging it might have shook the earth. Isabelle came up behind me, wrapping her arms over my shoulders as her heart pounded into my chest.

"I've never felt anger like this before, Izzy. I feel like I'm going out of my fucking mind," I said.

"Just breathe," she said. "Keep breathing steady breaths, Jack."

She reached out for my head. I noticed that she still wore her delicate white gloves. She pulled me into her chest and stroked my hair. She ran her fingers up and down the back my neck. She rocked me while I broke down in her arms and wailed. She rocked me while I cried. She rocked me while I coughed up phlegm and got it all over the place. And she kept rocking me until my breath steadied and fell into rhythm with her beating heart.

I dropped my head and cried some more. I whimpered like a child, a tired helpless child. Then the anger pummeled out of my body and the muffled tears turned to heavy sobs. Spit and snot covered my face. I snarled and hissed, then collapsed and my body hunched forward over my knees.

Izzy wiped my mouth with her thumb and I caught hold of her hand. I touched the white glove. I tapped the tiny pearl button clasp. I held her hand and looked into her eyes. Our sight locked.

"Just breathe," she said, rising up on her knees to face me.

I nodded, taking her gloves off one by one.

"Breathe," she whispered. Her soft lips settled on my ear. The warmth of her breath sent trickling pulses down my spine.

I clutched the back of her neck and tilted her lips toward mine. I pressed my lips against hers, knocking my tongue against her teeth until she opened her mouth and let me in. Isabelle kissed like a force. I clung to each throb of her lips against mine. We rolled back behind the bushes. I twisted out of my dinner jacket and threw it down on the ground as a blanket. I pressed my weight against her and we relaxed down onto the ground. I laid in between her knees and made a trail of kisses across her collarbone, a trail that she steered me along with her gliding fingertips.

I pushed every ounce of frustration through me that night, trying to find a more satisfying place to distract me. And that place was Isabelle. She rolled over, mounted herself on top of me and pulled up her dress. She reached underneath and took a firm hold of me, then pushed herself downward. I reached up underneath her dress and gripped her upper thighs. She wiggled her body in little circles until she was sitting all the way against me.

"Show me more of you," I called out in between gasps of air.

She reached behind her back and unzipped her dress, letting the shoulders fall down. She popped her round breasts out of her white cotton bra then bounced up and down, sending them jiggling in the air. Holy shit, I thought, in disbelief at how close I was to them. Then she tilted her body forward and there they were dangling in front of my eyes.

"Is this your first time, Jack?" she said.

"Yeah," I kind of yelped as I squirmed underneath her, not sure what the hell I was supposed to be doing. Never thinking she would be bouncing up and down on me like she was riding some sort of pogo stick or something.

"Hold my hips, Jack. Hold them nice and snug and kind of pull me back and forth."

"Ok, Iz," I said, my eyes going ga-ga over those fleshy mounds that grazed my face every time she drove herself upward.

I did what she said and in no time soon she was rolling over on her back and I was on top of her. She sunk her hands deep into my ass. Holy hell, I thought as I hovered over her, my hands clenching the rutted ground beneath her.

"Ride me, Jack," she said.

Was this some sort of Ferris wheel? Those phrases were new to my ears. But then Izzy's ride slowed down. She gurgled like she had something caught in her throat. A slow gurgle like when you're a kid blowing bubbles through a straw into a glass of pop and someone tells you to stop before it all spills over. But Izzy wasn't stopping, and pretty soon the strange noises from her mouth spilled out into the air between us. She panted like a dog, she purred like a cat, then she went hog wild and let out squeaks and squeals until at last, a trembling oooowww drooled from her lips and her body shuddered, then collapsed back against my jacket. I came to a sudden halt. My god, I thought, I've killed her. I stared at her face for a second with my eyes wide and my jaw dropped. Then Izzy's lips curled up and she released a slow breath. She fluttered her eyelids open and gave me one hell of a smile.

"Mmmh," she purred, rolling with me onto our sides. "Did you come, Jack?" she said as she scooted her backside up against me and pulled my arm down over her waist to cradle her from behind.

"Um, yeah. Sure, Iz. I came," I said, reaching down and yanking my pants up over my rock hard boner. We lay still for a few minutes. I felt like I could barely breathe, like I was holding my breath underwater and there was so much further to swim. I wasn't sure I was ready to come up for air. All the times I'd laid in bed thinking about Isabelle and I'd come in a matter of minutes, and now that I was finally with her in the flesh, nothing happened. I shook my head baffled.

"Listen, Isabelle. I'm real sorry about earlier. I'm sorry you had to hear me talk like that, cursing and ranting," I said.

"Jack, sometimes people talk real ugly when they find themselves a part of something real ugly. I won't hold it against you. Do you feel better now, Jack?" she said, grazing my hand with her fingertips.

"Yeah, Iz. I do. Thanks." We stood and dressed ourselves, dusting off the sand and dirt, shaking it from our hair. It was weird to think of what had happened between us. It should have felt like everything changed in that moment, but really, nothing had changed at all.

"Hey, Iz," I said as we walked along the sandy path back to the Honeysuckle. "Did you get that marijuana from your father's briefcase?"

"Sure did. Want to head back down to the beach? It's not too late, you know. The bonfire might still be going on. Our folks won't be expecting us back to the Inn for some time now."

"Yeah, let's do that. I don't think I could go back now anyway." I tossed my arm around her shoulder and she rested her head against mine.

When we arrived on the beach there was nothing but a few dying embers left in the bonfire. Some couples were scattered along the coast, their bodies buried beneath blankets. We sank down into the sand at the water's edge. We kicked off our shoes and stretched out our legs. The lapping water flirted with our toes, until smaller waves crashed up over our calves.

We smoked a joint that Isabelle seemed to roll up in the matter of seconds. The waves blurred, the moon light found us, and then her voice trailed off to some far away place.

"I think I'm stoned," she said.

"I don't know about that," I said.

"Why, you don't think I am?"

"Well, when you're really stoned, your mind stops thinking. But you said *I think I'm stoned*, so maybe you aren't really stoned because you were thinking that you were stoned. So what do you think about that?"

"That's not fair, Jack! You're asking me to think!"

"Well, do you feel hungry? If you're really stoned then you would be real hungry, ravenous like. Are you hungry, Iz?"

A small laugh escaped her. "Yeah, Jack. I'm really hungry, like so hungry I think I saw some seaweed over there that I could eat. You want some?"

"Holy shit, Iz. You must be really stoned. I've never heard of anyone being so hungry that they would eat seaweed."

"Jack! I wouldn't eat seaweed, but if you said you were so hungry that you would go and eat seaweed, then I thought that would mean you were really stoned, too."

"There you go thinking again," I said, cracking myself up.

Izzy took a hit off the joint and flopped back on the sand, stretching her arms out wide.

"Jack."

"Yeah, Iz."

"I'm stoned."

"I knew it all along."

"Jack!" She rolled on top of me and started ticking my sides. She pressed her forehead up against mine and laughed and laughed. She laughed so hard tears fell out of her eyes and coated my face. For a second, I thought it was raining. Then her laughter settled into a pleasing sigh.

"Oh, Jack," she said, falling back onto the sand.

We lay next to one another for some time. I stretched my hand down beside me. I could see hers there too, palm up. I don't know why I was so shy about reaching down and holding it. I mean, after what we'd done earlier, reaching down and holding her hand shouldn't have felt like a big deal, but somehow it did.

"Hey, little brother." I felt a sharp kick beneath my ribs.

"What the hell, Thomas," I said, whacking his leg with the back of my arm. Leave it to Thomas to disrupt my moment of calm.

"I'm heading back to my room. Here's a few beers," he said, dropping some cans by my head. "I'm not going to drink them if you kids want 'em." He reached down and roughed up Isabelle's hair.

"Will you knock it off?" I said, swatting his hand away while Isabelle turned her head and smoothed her hair down.

Thomas snorted and walked away.

I cracked open a can of beer and sipped through the foam. I offered some to Izzy, but she shook her head no, so I drank it myself.

"I'm sleepy, Jack. Bedtime for me."

"Ok, Iz. But not before you tell me one thing."

"What's that?"

"Tell me one thing that stirs your soul?"

"Oh, Jack. Didn't you know?"

"Huh?"

"You."

"Me?" I smiled, then coughed, wondering if all of a sudden she was being sarcastic or joking or something.

"Sure you. We're having quite a time this summer, aren't we?"

"We sure are, Iz. We sure are. And there's only one week left. Can you believe it, Iz? We made it."

"We did, Jack Sullivan." She leaned over and pecked me on the cheek. "We made it together." She tweaked my nose and kissed the tip, then rose to her feet. "If you need a bed to sleep in, you know where to find me."

"Thanks, Izzy," I said, standing up, then bending back down for my beer. "Here let me walk you back."

"That's ok, Jack. I can manage."

"I insist, Isabelle."

"Alright, then."

"Hey, Iz," I said once we'd reached the Inn and I'd opened the back screen door.

"Yeah, Jack."

"I want you to start insisting upon things for yourself, too, ok? I mean not just now, here, but always. You deserve someone to walk you home." She lowered her head. "You're a lady, Isabelle Whitney. People should always treat you like one."

"Well, then I'd better start acting like one!" she laughed, taking the can out of my hand and slurping the beer before waving goodnight. She walked away, a trail of hiccups left echoing in her path. I watched her shuffle down the hall. Her elbow was raised real high. She must've been pressing the back of her hand to her mouth to cover up the hiccups. This seemed to only send her giggling each time one escaped her. I shook my head and smiled, then turned to head back down the hill and toward the beach.

I thought of Isabelle during my walk. I often felt like she was caught acting a part that wasn't really her. She was lady-like, Isabelle was. She was gorgeous, and polished, and charming. She was also smart as a whip, and witty, and well, kind of one of the guys. I think that worked for her at times and against her at others. Izzy was that girl next door, the one you've known all your life, the type that for one reason or another men outgrow when they become older, but rarely grow out of, the girl that is always there knocking about in your head after you've surfaced into the world of women. She's the one a memory always goes back to, and a heart never forgets. I was glad that I'd treated her like a lady and ended well our night together.

I cracked open another can of beer from the pack and dangled the rest from my finger. It felt good to be alone. Being with Isabelle had been a nice distraction, and welcomed at that, but I needed time to digest the reality of my father. Hell, I always knew he wasn't a great man, but seeing that in the flesh, quite literally, was a lot to handle.

I decided to stay on the Honeysuckle's great lawn, not even feeling up for the walk over the dunes and to the beach. I let my body collapse on the grass. I lay there, sprawled out on my back. I moved my limbs up and down like I was making a snow angel, then I closed my eyes. I only lifted my head to swig beer from the can, only lifted my arm when it meant chucking a smashed empty down the hill. I'd cried all my tears out earlier on the sandy road. I'd let all my frustration loose back there, too. There was nothing left. My mind just slipped into a white space. It felt like there were no thoughts left to entertain, even though the weight of the world seemed to be pressing my body down against the ground, pressing it down like it were trying to make some sort of grave for me and bury me in the earth.

WAKE-UP CALL

"Wake up, Jack Sullivan. You've got work to do," a voice said, jabbing my arm with a pointed finger.

"Maybelle? Is that you? My god, Maybelle, what time is it?" I said, rubbing my eyes and rising up onto my elbows. I looked all around me. I made sight of her frame behind me, but her body kept going in and out of focus. Her face was getting real large, then real small, like a balloon when you're blowing it up, and every time you stop and take a breath so you can give it some more air, the whole thing deflates on you.

"Five-thirty in the morning. You look a mess, Jack Sullivan. What on earth happened to you last night?" Her hands were on her hips now, I could see that much from the little triangles that formed between her elbows and her waistline.

I squinted. Now her head was shaking, or was it? Hell, I couldn't tell.

"C'mon now, get up on your feet. We've got to get you cleaned up before your parents have a fit," she said, bracing my body and lifting me up. She took hold of my arm, then began dragging me over the grass as she trudged her munchkin feet up the hill.

"Didn't I ever tell you I wasn't your rag doll?" I laughed, remembering back to the first time we'd met.

"Oh, for the love! What am I going to do with you?" she laughed along, then let go of my shirt and waved her hand for me to walk faster. "Pick up your feet, Jack. Hurry up, now. I can't have anyone finding me hauling your behind back to the Inn at this hour of the morning."

But I couldn't help it. The way my feet kept sticking to the ground, you would have thought there was honey covering the soles. Anyway, I loved that time of morning, and the sun was blazing red as it rose beside the Inn. I slipped into a quiet daydream and felt my walk getting slower again.

Maybelle made *tsk* sounds and shook her head, then trudged up the hill without me. I suppose it was enough that she'd woken me up. I couldn't blame her. Walking behind her, I saw that Maybelle was wearing the same dress she'd worn last night when

I'd helped her push the hors d'oeuvres cart into the parlor. And out of the corner of my eye, I saw that band player, the one Maybelle'd been talking to last night when Izzy and I'd snuck back inside. There he was hunkering down and creeping up the other side of the hill toward the parking lot.

I caught up to Maybelle.

"You have a good night, Jack?" she said, huffing and puffing.

"Had its ups and downs," I said. "You?"

"Well now, I do believe it was one of the better times I've had while stuck working at this place." Her eyes glimmered at the sky and her sight traveled to some far off place.

Seeing that look in Maybelle's eyes as she stared off at the sky, why, it made me wish I could find my way to that place, too. But then I recalled I had. It was the day that Izzy and I had hitched a ride back from Provincetown. It was the moment she'd rested her head on my shoulder, traced circles on my hand, hummed her folk songs, and made her purring sounds. It happened as I watched out the window, and felt the wind on my face, blowing so hard I had to strain to keep my eyes open. But then the car had stopped at a flashing red light, and the wind had come to a lull, and I'd stared out at the sky, that fucking blue sky. It had been such a clear blue, crystal like. I'd stared so hard at the sky that day, hell, I thought I was looking straight through it, right through to the other side. And then the Portuguese grandmother had pressed her foot on the gas, picking up speed, and so did the wind as it barreled through the car. And I had closed my eyes, and when I had, the vision in front of me was Isabelle; I was home.

Maybelle brought me to. "Jack, you need to clean yourself up now. We're running a little late this morning, and there's no way I'm going to find time to clean up the parlor, make the breakfast, and get them papers. You've got thirty minutes to ready yourself and get on down there to the mailbox, you here?"

"Yes, ma'am," I said, snapping back to reality as we walked up the back steps to the Inn and I rushed upstairs to change.

I found it funny that Maybelle said we, when she should have been saying I. But I felt somehow flattered, as though she knew I was different from the others, as if she could tell I was on her team and not theirs. And so I was happy to oblige my duties as the Honeysuckle Inn Sunday paper boy.

I took the stairs two at a time, and that time around I didn't give a damn if anyone saw me coming into the Inn so early in the morning. Unlike the first day, impressions didn't matter much to me anymore. When I reached my bedroom door, I put my hand real slow on the brass knob. I felt like I was in a horror movie, not knowing what was going to be waiting for me on the other side, or like I was on a crime show, playing the detective and revisiting the scene, except there was no yellow tape warning me to stay back. I pushed the door open inch by inch. Chills ran through my bones as if spirits were surrounding me. How many other people's lives were destroyed in this room, I thought as my body shivered and shook.

I needed to make my way into the bathroom. I wanted to wash up before going down to get the papers. My skin smelled. My breath was foul. When I ran my tongue over my teeth they were layered with grime.

Part of me expected to walk in the bathroom and see Father going at it again. The other part of me expected to find him passed out cold. I was fearful that I'd have to crawl over their wrinkled bodies to reach the sink. But when I pushed back the door, I saw nothing. The only thing that I saw were the cigarette ashes scattered all over the tiles and a lone cigarette butt floating in the toilet. I stared at the cigarette floating in the toilet water and felt my stomach collapse. The filter was brown. The filters on my cigarettes were white. I flushed it down, took out my mouthwash, gargled and spit. I was afraid to use the toothbrush I'd left on the counter for fear that one of them had used it. I splashed water on my face, then puked up whatever acids were left attacking my stomach. I put my head under the faucet and let the water stream over my face and down over my eyes as I tried to cleanse myself of all that I had seen.

I turned back to face the scene as I shut the door. I gathered every speck of spit in my mouth and heaved the biggest phlegm wad I could muster smack dab on the middle of the marble bathroom floor. Then I closed the door.

I took the steps down the stairs two at a time down, then dashed out the front door, tucking in my shirt as I ran down toward the mailbox. The sun gave off pinkish orange hues. The gulls were making music for me as I walked to my post by the mailbox. I walked in circles, kicking up dirt while I waited. Then I heard the loud thunderclap of the truck as it rounded the bed. This time I didn't jump.

"Morning, son," the man yelled out from the driver seat as he slammed the shift stick into park.

The newspaper girl's arm reached over the passenger side door, pulling up the handle. I reached out for the door and opened it for her.

"Good morning, Jack. It's Jack, isn't it? Was kind of hard to hear as we drove away last time," she said.

I walked with her to the back of the truck. "Yes, that's right. Here let me get those for you." I hopped up onto the bumper and heaved the pile of papers up and over the truck, then dropped it down on the lawn.

"Just the one pile, Jenny?" I said. "Jenny, right?"

"Yes," she said, lowering her head. "Just the one."

"There now." I extended my hand. "I'm Jack Sullivan."

"Jenny Joslin."

"It's real nice to meet you, Jenny." I reached down and hoisted the papers up in my arms. I walked with her to the passenger door. She hopped in, then blushed as she watched my hand press the metal handle down for her. I closed the door.

"Mr. Joslin?" I said.

"Yes, son," he said.

"Sir, I'm Jack Sullivan. I'm a guest here at the Inn and Maybelle's Sunday helper."

"Nice to formally meet you, son."

"Sir, I'll only be here another week, but if you and Jenny would like," I said, looking into her caramel brown eyes, "why don't you be our guests at breakfast next Sunday after your route."

Jenny's eyes rose like the sun. "I'd like that, Jack. Daddy?" she said, turning and dipping her head toward her father. "Daddy, I'd like that very much." Her voice quieted.

"Why thank you, son. Mighty kind of you. We'll be done by seven sharp," he said.

"Thank you, Jack," Jenny said. "We'll look forward to it!" She reached her hand out and placed it on top of mine. I found her gesture endearing. I tried to balance the stack of papers in my hand, tipping them into my side. She blushed again, then slid her hand away as I rescued the teetering paper pile by clenching it real tight with both hands. Her father made a rumbling sound in his throat. Jenny crossed her hands in front of her lap, her fingers loosely tangled, and gushed a smile. I couldn't help but smile back.

"I'll see you Sunday," I said.

"See you then," she whispered, and the truck sputtered on.

It might seem funny that I was asking another girl and her father to have breakfast with me on the morning after being with Isabelle. Though, I did so with no intentions, except to offer them a sort of thank-you for their delivery service as I couldn't imagine old lady Gardenia going out of her way to do so. Hell, I was sure Ms. Gardenia probably didn't even know who delivered the Sunday papers at all. She probably thought they fell right out of the sky and glided to a landing on the front steps of the Honeysuckle. I also invited them because on those few occasions that I had caught sight of Jenny Joslin, I'd felt a funny spark inside me, like I was soaring up in the clouds, heading in new directions. I'd never felt that spark before, and I began to believe that what I'd felt was the spark of hope. I had needed a lot of it in the beginning of the summer and I needed a lot more of it now. I was grateful for the light in Jenny Joslin's eyes.

I lugged the pile of papers up the steps. They fell with a plunk and I let the screen door slam shut nice and loud, the way Maybelle liked. Maybelle leaned back at the waist from where she stood at the counter cracking eggs into a large yellow bowl.

92

"Thank you, Jack," she said.

"My pleasure, Maybelle," I said.

I walked back around to the front lawn, went through the doorway and up the stairs. I was headed for Isabelle's room, not wanting to step back into my own. As I walked down the hall, I saw my mother coming out of her room. Her narrow shoulders trembled. Her face was blotchy and red. Her eyes were puffy. Mascara was smeared beneath her eyes and she pawed away at it in a frenetic way that resembled anyone other than the tranquil mother I knew.

"Pack your bags, Jack, and meet me by the car. We're headed home," she said.

"What?" I said.

"Don't ask me any questions. Just pack your bags and do as I say. We'll get breakfast on the way. I'll explain in the car."

"When?"

"Now, Jack. Right now. I don't want to run into a living soul around here. I've been lying awake praying for daylight to come so I could just leave this place. Please, pack your bags right away. Pack your bags and come straight out to the car."

Mother walked down the stairs, one hand pressed flat against her stomach. She went into the room connected off the far end of the parlor, the same room where I'd brought Isabelle on the morning I'd found her in bad shape on the beach. It was Maybelle's room and now Mother was there.

I'd been sucker punched before, hard not to have been when you've got a goon like Thomas for a brother. But the feeling that filled up my stomach at that moment was inexplicable. Did I want to stay at the Honeysuckle Inn? Hell, no. But did I want to leave? Well, no, not really. On the day that I hated the place the most, I also loved the place the most. I had a best friend in Isabelle Whitney, a real soul mate, and after July we'd go our separate ways, and when the hell would I see her again? I needed time with her, just one more day lying out on the beach talking our nonsense, one more time listening to her hum her folk songs, or kiss the tip of my nose, one more time for me to sling my arm over her shoulder, call her Izzy or Iz, sneak cans of beer on the beach, puff

93

on one another's cigarettes, and make moonlight confessions of what stirred our souls alive. Goddamit, I just wanted one more day. I brooded. I paced up and down the hall. I hunched my shoulders and stomped with each step, and she must have known, because of all the doors to open a crack, peek out and see what was the matter, it was hers.

Izzy pulled me inside her room and sat me down on her bed. She cradled me and listened to me as I blubbered away in her arms. When I wiped my snot on my shirt sleeve, she smiled and kissed my forehead and told me to "Breathe, Jack. Just breathe." And I caught my breath, and I breathed.

"Ah, shit, Izzy. I think I love you," I said.

"I know, Jack," she said, throwing back her covers, scooting inside, and pulling me close to her. We faced one another, eye to eye, mouth to mouth.

"But I've never loved anybody, Iz. So I don't know if this is it or not. What do you think?"

She smiled through a mouthful of tears. "I'm not sure what form it's taken or what shape it is, but I do think it's love, Jack."

"Oh, Jack," she said, her delicate fingertips quivering against her lips as she whimpered. "I love you, too. I guess I never thought that someday you just wouldn't be there. My dearest friend, just gone." She grabbed my face with both hands and stared at with me with panic stricken through her eyes. "You promise you'll write me back when I write you, Jack? Promise?"

"I promise, Iz." But my heart grew sad at the thought of writing her miles away and not being there to see the light on her face when I wrote something funny, not feeling her punch me in the arm when I said something crass, not holding her close when she got tipsy and wanted to talk my ear off all night.

"Oh god, my heart hurts, Iz. I feel like I'm dying, really dying. Oh god, make it stop." I reached out and held her for dear life.

We sobbed. I mean real sobs. The kind of sobs that Thomas and Father would smack me around about. But oh god, I couldn't help it. Because in my heart, I knew, deep down in that part of you that knows the truth about life, about what comes and goes,

I knew that the chances of me ever spending time like this again with Isabelle were one in a million. And my heart broke because for the first time in my life I realized that time, time passes. It fucking passes, and goddamnit it doesn't ask you if you're ready or if it's alright. It doesn't check with you at all. And my heart bled there in her arms as I cursed time, because all I wanted was more of my sweet Isabelle, more home, and it was going. It was gone.

'TILL DEATH DO THEM PART

I knocked on the door to Maybelle's room. She opened it a crack and waved me in.

"Excuse me, Maybelle. I'm sorry to bother you, but is my mother here?" I said, hoisting my packed duffle bag up over my shoulder.

"She's out at the car, Jack. It's all loaded up. She wants to leave before the morning breakfast crowd comes down," Maybelle said.

I looked over and saw Mother's robe on Maybelle's bed post. "Did Mother sleep her here last night, Maybelle?"

"She did, Jack."

"I know why we're going home, Maybelle. Do you know why we're going home?" I unzipped my bag and stuffed Mother's robe down inside.

"I can't be too sure, Jack."

"My father was with another woman last night, Maybelle. Does Mother know that?"

"Why, Jack. I'm not able to say. Your mother will tell you what she wants to tell you, when she wants to tell you. You're a good boy, Jack Sullivan. You've been good to me all summer long. You've shown your manners when they've mattered the most, not just when it was a matter of convenience. That there is a sign of a true gentleman, and a gentleman is what I'm sure you are. So be gentle with your momma. She's going to need it."

"She'll just die now that she knows," I said, yanking the zipper of my duffel bag closed. I sank down onto Maybelle's mattress. I buried my head in between my hands and burned my gaze into the floor.

"She won't die, Jack. Knowing the truth might be the only thing to save your momma, bring her back to life."

"And what if they split up, Maybelle? It'll just about be the end of her. My mother's a religious woman. All those vows about 'till death do us part, that kind of stuff. I'm telling you, it's going to destroy her."

"You've grown up around here these past weeks, Jack. I've seen it in you, the way you study the world around you, trying to make sense of it all. Well, you can try to make sense of those wedding vows too, if you'd like; I know I have. But those vows that you're speaking of, who is to say what the death is that does the people part? To one person, death might be when your father's heart stops ticking and he's physically dead and gone. But your father's heart might have stopped ticking for your momma a long time ago. It seems your father's heart ticks only for himself, wouldn't you say?"

"I would."

"And all of that nonsense your father does, whatever it may be, behind closed doors, what if all that is killing your momma? There may be parts of your momma that you never knew about, Jack. Beautiful parts. Parts of her that *are* dead and gone. And ain't that a parting out of death in some way, Jack? Now don't you think that maybe it is? So those vows might have some truth to 'em after all. It's all in the way you think 'em through."

I stared at Maybelle mystified. Maybelle walked over to me, took my duffel bag off my shoulder and placed it at the foot of the bed. She sat down next to me, held both of my hands in hers, and with each word she spoke she gave each one a tender squeeze.

"Your momma's got *soul* there in her eyes. And it probably once flickered as fierce as the light I've seen dancing in your eyes since that first morning you done wandered into my kitchen! Such a good boy, you are, Jack. Such a good boy. And your momma is a mighty good woman."

"Thank you, Maybelle. Thank you." I reached over and took hold of my duffel bag, throwing it back over my shoulder as I leaned in and hugged her good-bye. I headed for the door, then turned around.

"Excuse me, Maybelle. There is something that I'm going to need to ask of you."

"Anything, Jack."

"I need you to tell the Joslins, the paper folks, that I had to leave early. I invited them as guests to breakfast next Sunday, and I'm terribly sorry that I won't be here to host them."

"I'll make sure to let them know. Why I'll call the daddy tonight, see if they would still like to come, but explain you won't be here. They're good people, Jack. They'll understand."

"And I'm sorry I won't be around here any longer to help you out on Sundays, Maybelle."

"I'll miss you're help for sure, Jack."

"I'm really going to miss you, Maybelle," I said, taking in a sharp breath.

"Jack Sullivan, the pleasure has been mine."

HOME IS WHERE THE HURT IS

I went through the kitchen and out the back door. I ran my fingers up and down the screen, holding the door tight in my hand so it didn't make a sound when it shut. I crammed my hands into my pocket, feeling around to make sure the scrap of paper with Isabelle's address was still in there. I walked over to the car. Should I act like I didn't know anything? Foolish, I thought. Just tell her if it comes up.

"You can sit in the front, Jack," Mother said, locking the trunk and going around to the driver's seat.

"What about Father and Thomas?" I said.

"They're staying until the end of the week. They'll come home together on the weekend. Then Thomas will pack up and be off to Cambridge the following week. He has to go up early for football. I told you I'd explain everything in the car, and now I have. There's a lot to be done before you kids start school again. No sense wasting any more time around here." She rolled down the window. I reached under the passenger seat and pulled out her cigarettes, lighting two of them. Brown filters. Ah, shit, I thought.

After only a mile or so from the Inn, Mother laid into the horn. A few short blasts followed by a series of long drawn out ones.

"You can scream if you want to, Mother. It might feel good," I said, thinking she was using the horn to purge her wrath.

"Now why would I want to do something like that, Jack?" she said.

"It's ok to get angry, Mother."

"Nothing to be angry about, Jack."

"Then why are we leaving a week early if you aren't mad about something?" I flicked my ashes out the window, but they flew back in the car at me.

"Like I said, Jack, I only wanted to go home and get things ready for the new school year. You should see how many pairs of your pants have sand caked into the creases. And don't even get me started on Thomas' clothes. I'll need those all pressed by the time he leaves for Harvard. It's just housekeeping, Jack. I thought you'd be happy to join me. Have a little extra time at home with your friends while summer is still in full swing."

"Ok," I said, puffing on my cigarette and biting the filter. I kind of felt like chewing it off or smoking the wrong end and burning my tongue. Crazy thoughts, I know, but I was living in a world of crazy, so it seemed.

When we pulled into our driveway in Ithaca, I felt relieved to be home. I felt around for the house key in the bottom of the mailbox, opened the door, and bee lined for my room. I threw my bag into the closet, didn't bother to unpack it, then lay down on my bed and inhaled the musty, muggy air before drifting asleep.

*****

The week at home dragged. Mother did the laundry, and then some, washing every piece of fabric throughout the entire house. The couches, the carpets, hell, if it was washable then she was on her hands and knees scrubbing it clean. The house was the best I had ever remembered it looking, not that I'd spent too much time contemplating how clean the house was growing up, but still, it was pretty damn spotless.

The night before Father and Thomas came home, Mother made batches of cookies. Why you might have thought it was Christmas. She said they were for Thomas to take to school with him, which struck me as odd because in the past all she'd ever sent back with Thomas was a loaf of Wonder bread and a few jars of peanut butter.

The morning that Thomas and Father were heading back from the Cape, Mother set the table for lunch. I played solitaire at the kitchen table, and when she was done folding the napkins, Mother sat down, too. She drank her coffee, and chain-smoked her cigarettes. She pushed the chair back against the floor every ten minutes or so and stared out the kitchen window in search of the town car that would bring Father and Thomas home from the train station in Syracuse. Father insisted on having a car service drive them from Syracuse, even though it was only an hour drive. Mother rolled her eyes as she told me that Father wanted to arrive home to Ithaca in style.

100

"They're here," Mother said. The rattle of her voice nearly knocked me off my seat.

I walked into the kitchen, contemplating whether or not I should go out and help them with their bags. Mother stayed glued to the kitchen window, fumbling with the end of her cigarette. After a minute, she crushed out the butt in the ashtray, and ran her tongue over her teeth.

I looked out the window and saw Father wrestling with a suitcase in the trunk. It struck me then that I didn't know if Father knew I'd been the one to walk in on him that night in the bathroom. But who the hell else would it have been? I hadn't bothered to find him to say goodbye when Mother and I had left the Honeysuckle. My mouth went real dry and my stomach sunk when I heard the trunk door slam shut. He was home.

Father hurried through the kitchen door, his suitcase up in the air. "Sport!" he said. "We missed you last week! You would have loved it. Ms. Gardenia had another fireworks display and a clambake on the beach. We all thought of you." He slapped my back. Every time he slapped my back it was all I could do from punching his lights out.

Father trotted over to Mother who stuck out her cheek as he planted a big kiss right on her with the same lips that he had used to kiss the watermelon pink nipples on the Honeysuckle whore. I gagged and puke filled my mouth.

"You alright, son?" Father glared at me.

I nodded.

"Answer your father, Jack," Mother said, opening the refrigerator and removing turkey cold cuts from the meat drawer.

Father waited for my response, staring at me like he was daring me to not answer him. I swallowed hard, then reached for my glass of water near the kitchen sink, swishing it around my mouth before responding. "Yes, sir. I'm fine."

"That's what I thought," he said, sneering. "Stupid kid," he muttered as he walked down the hall.

My whole body froze. Who the hell was he talking about, *me*? Had he thought I was out of earshot? Had he thought that I hadn't heard? Waves of shock rolled through my shoulders and chest, and everything got real tight. My body felt a little fried, a little empty, and I wondered if I'd been electrocuted or something because my mind started to feel a little empty, too.

"Mother!" Thomas said, dropping his bags on the welcome mat as she ran over and hugged him.

"I've made dozens of cookies, Thomas. Chocolate chip, your favorite. You can pass them around the dorm. Your laundry is clean and pressed and all packed in your luggage upstairs. Leave your dirty clothes in the basement and you can add any of the other clothes you need later on."

She loaded the bread up with slabs of meat and spread gobs of mayonnaise over the top pieces before slicing the sandwiches diagonally. She poured four tall glasses of whole milk. We sat eating and listening to one another chew. Mother's chewing was inaudible, Thomas' was grotesque, and Father's was damn right annoying, hell with the way he smacked his mouth about with each bite. The meals at the Honeysuckle were bearable in that there was always something in the dining room to distract us. Here, in our suburban kitchen, there was nothing to divert our attention. We were forced to pay attention to one another during the dreadful encounter until the meal was over. I wiped my forehead with my napkin. I thought my sweat would make a puddle on my plate.

Father glugged the last of his milk and pushed his plate away from him. "What a long day. I'm going up stairs to take a nap. Wake me for dinner, Claire," Father said. "Remember boys, no horseplay in the house."

Thomas and I looked at each other and shrugged our shoulders. I couldn't remember the last time Thomas and I had played anything together in the house, least of all roughhousing.

"Hey, little brother," Thomas snickered as he pulled his duffel bag along the ground and kicked it down the basement stairs. "Isabelle Whitney asked that I say hello to you."

"Thanks for the message," I said as Mother patted my shoulder, then excused herself to the other room.

102

"What a rack on that one, huh?" Thomas said.

I rolled my eyes, the last thing I wanted to do was talk about my Izzy with Thomas.

"What a prude, though," he said. "I had to hold her down that first week just to get in a good feel. You know what I'm saying?" He sunk his teeth down into his sandwich. A trail of crumbs coated his upper lip and a glob of mayonnaise rested in the corner of his mouth.

"No, Thomas. I really don't know what the hell you're saying," I said, pushing my chair away from the table, and then slamming my plate into the sink. I'd be glad when the time came for Thomas to grab his packed bags and head back to Harvard for the semester.

"Mother?" Thomas called.

"Yes?" she said, scurrying back into the kitchen and looking around as if something were the matter.

"My clothes that you packed, how did you fold them? Did you fold both shirt arms back to meet each other so the crease is down the line of the buttons? Or did you fold them the other idiotic way, where you fold them back one at a time with the shirt facing you, then fold it over again, leaving a crease across the center?"

"Thomas, I folded the shirts as I always fold them."

"Well, that's just great, Mother. Now I'll have to spend my first night home refolding my damn clothes!" he said.

Mother and I looked at each other. I didn't know what to think about the whole episode, but flickers of Thomas' childhood tantrums flashed through my mind. Mother took in a long, slow breath and I crinkled my face. I shook my head, then excused myself outside where I went for a walk around the neighborhood.

That night, I laid in my twin bed just inches away from where Thomas slept in his bed. While I laid there, I contemplated all the ways I could hurt Thomas in his sleep for the crude comments he'd made about Izzy and for the foul way he'd spoken to Mother. But my thoughts were distracted by the muffled sobs coming from the end of the hall.

I watched the hand of the clock on the wall until an hour had passed. The sobs were still there; they were Mothers for sure. I had to pee so bad that I thought my bladder would burst. But getting up to pee meant going down the hall next to my parents' room and I became paralyzed with fear at the thought. I didn't want Mother to know that I'd heard her so upset. I didn't want to be brought into the whole thing at all. So I lay there thinking of all the possible solutions, until at last, I tiptoed across the room, inched the zipper back real slow on Thomas' luggage, and took the most satisfying piss I had ever remembered all over his perfectly refolded back to school clothes. Then back into bed I crawled and fell asleep.

*****

A week later, we waved Thomas off as Father drove him to the Syracuse train station to catch the one o'clock to Boston. I chugged the last of the orange juice from the carton left on the counter. Mother cleared the morning dishes. Even though it was a solid few hours before Father would return, it seemed like only a matter of minutes before we heard the Studebaker roll back into the driveway and the car door slam shut.

"Why the hell is it so hot in here?" Father said as he stormed through the kitchen door.

"It's August, Harv," Mother said, cranking open the windows.

"Well if it's August, *Claire*, then why the hell aren't the fans out? You've been home an entire week and what do you have to show for it? You can't even bring down a couple of fans from the attic to cool the damn place down? After a long trip home like the one I had to make last week, because you just *had* to leave the Honeysuckle early and leave us stranded there, and you couldn't even bring down a couple of fans? Honestly, Claire, what good are you?" Father cursed his way up to the attic where he banged things around.

"Mother?" I said.

"Yes, Jack," she said.

"Mother, are you going to let him talk to you like that?"

"Like what, Jack?"

104

"Like *that*."

"It's fine, Jack. I'm fine. Run along now."

And so I did run along, out of the house, down past the high school and around the old track where I got in a good two miles before I cooled down. Running around the track hammered into my conscience the nagging sense that I hadn't noticed a whole world happening in my house for the past seventeen years. Bits of memory flew at me as I ran. The countless meals where Father bitched about the pancakes being too cold, the bread buttered the wrong way, the toast cut in triangles instead of squares, the coffee that was too bitter, the coffee that was too sweet. Goddamn, that old bastard had a word of criticism for everything. I remembered all those times when Mother would leave the table, coming back with watery eyes and blaming her allergies. All those times when that asshole had made her cry. Why he had a comment for everything, my father did. Hell, he'd probably walk into someone else's bathroom and tell them they were wiping their own ass the wrong way if he had the chance.

I jogged back home and ran up the stairs, heading straight for the shower. I let the water run for a while. The bathroom filled with hot steam. I wrote my initials on the mirror. I liked the steam. In a foggy world, it made my mind feel more clear.

Father must have thought that the shower water would drown out everything. He must have thought I wouldn't hear. But would you believe that my old man had the gall to tell my mother that she'd deserved it. I pressed my ear to the door. It sounded like he was standing in the hall, probably outside their bedroom door.

"Maybe if you'd had sex with me more than once a week, I wouldn't have had to do what I did, Claire. You were asking for this all summer, and now you've gotten it, so don't go blubbering away over the whole thing. You're a lazy piece of shit, Claire. You're goddamned lazy with the house, you're lazy with the boys, and you're lazy with me. What kind of wife are you? An alright one, but not a great one, that's for sure. Goddamit Claire, I should have known what I was getting into when I married a Vassar girl. My mother warned me you'd find some reason to think you were better than me if you had an education under your belt. I should have stuck with my first girlfriend.

Goddamn, I'd be getting hot sex *and* hot meals, two things you never seemed to get the hang of making. Look at you Claire, just *look* at you. Could you blame me?"

Mother bawled.

I curled up on the cold bathroom floor. I rocked myself back and forth and sobbed. This house was no longer my home. I cried out for Isabelle.

EVERY DAY, BUT NEVER

The next morning Father left for work at the usual time. I walked downstairs to find Mother standing in her robe by the kitchen sink, sipping her coffee and staring out the window. When she turned to look at me I discovered that her right eye was a dark yellow with a rim of brown surrounding it. An empty gaze washed over her face.

"Good morning, Jack. Pancakes or waffles?" she said.

"Mother?" I said.

"Or I can save the batter for tomorrow and do eggs today. Your choice. What'll it be?"

"Mother, your eye. What happened?" I said, gripping the back of the kitchen chair with white knuckles.

"Oh, Jack, just a little black and blue."

"Father?" I said, wobbling on my feet, afraid I was going to crash to the floor.

"Oh, I don't know," she said. "How about scrambled eggs *and* pancakes! That's what I'll make you. A lumberjack breakfast for my little lumberjack!"

"Mother!"

"Jack, why are you raising your voice at me?"

"Because you're acting like a robot and I want my mother." My voice trembled. My body shuddered as if I had a fever. It shook so fast I couldn't stop it.

Mother stood there like a statue. The bewildered expression on her face was stiff as stone. The spatula in her hand began shaking, slow at first then real fast. Seeing her like that, well I couldn't help but lose control of myself.

"Jack, why are you crying?"

"Because I want my mother!" I cried, sinking to the floor. "I want my mother."

Mother's legs buckled and she fell down beside me.

"Jack, I'm not a robot. I'm right here, sweetheart. I'm right here." She reached out and put her arm around me, sheltering me from the reality of our home life.

"Then answer me, Mother. Did Father do that to you?"

She looked at me with the fear of a child stranded in a store and separated from their parent. She looked at me like she didn't know what she was supposed to do, or how to ask for help.

"You need to tell me, Mother. Did he do that to you?"

"Yes, Jack. He did. Does that change anything?"

"It should, Mother. Shouldn't it? Shouldn't it change everything? I heard the way he yelled at you last night, and the night before that. Has he always talked to you like that? Have I just never heard it?"

"He's never talked to me in front of you like that, not until now, Jack. I'm not sure why he's begun acting like this in front of you, but he has."

I knew why, but I didn't tell her. Father must have known it had been me that had walked in on him in my bathroom at the Honeysuckle. I had caught a glimpse of the monster that night, and there was nothing left for him to hide.

"Why haven't you ever left him, Mother?" I said.

"Jack, leaving your father was something that I promised myself I would do every day of my life since he began mistreating me."

"Well, what happened?"

"I never did."

"But you wanted to?"

"Every day, Jack. Every day, but never."

LOST THEN FOUND

"Pack your bags, Jack," Mother said as she nudged me awake the next morning. The black of night peeked through my window.

"Mother?" I whispered.

"It's not permanent, Jack. I don't think I have that much courage, yet. Just a vacation. We deserve it."

"But didn't we just get back from a vacation?"

"From *their* vacation, Jack. Now let's go on ours."

I hadn't put away any of the clothes from the Honeysuckle trip. They were still wadded in my luggage at the bottom of my closet. My laziness made the packing real easy. I just snatched up my bag and crept downstairs.

I found Father sitting in the dark at the kitchen table which just about gave me a heart attack. Mother hadn't said if this was some sort of covert mission, and I feared I'd just blown our getaway.

Father cleared his throat. "The tank is full, Jack. I'd appreciate it if you drove the car there. Your mother's feeling, well, a bit *fragile,* shall we say. Women get like that from time to time. You just have to ride it out." He shook his head and sneered.

I couldn't move from the kitchen doorway. I couldn't take my eyes off of his pathetic scowl. I couldn't shake that sarcastic tone he'd used about my mother.

"I saw you, Father," I said.

"Sure, Jack. Whatever. Now remember, don't let the gas tank get below a quarter full."

"I saw you. I saw you on the bathroom floor. The bathroom floor in my room at the Honeysuckle."

"I'm not sure what you mean, Jack. Who knows what anyone saw at that place. Everyone was two sheets to the wind, yourself included, and don't think I didn't notice, young man."

"I saw you screwing that woman, Father. And I heard you screaming at Mother. And I've seen her eye."

Father swatted his hand into the air as if to say my talk was all nonsense.

"I saw you, Father, and I see you. I see you for exactly the person you are. So enough with the charades from now on. No more. A bit fragile? Is that what you called her?"

"Well, yes, Jack," Father said, swallowing hard. "And you'd do best to keep whatever it is you imagine you found while snooping around to yourself. You don't want to upset your mother any further, do you?"

Mother walked into the room, switched on the light, and grabbed her purse off the counter. She stared back and forth between me and Father.

"Everything alright in here?" she said.

"Fine, Claire."

"Fine, Mother."

"Ok, then. Let's go, Jack. Harv, we'll see you in three weeks."

A small twitch flared up beneath Father's eye, and before long, spasms were erupting all over the whole left side of his face. "Well, ok, then. Alright. Have fun you two. Enjoy your second vacation while some of us have to work around here!" Father said, walking behind us out the door.

"Oh, we will, Harv!" Mother said, shuffling down the sidewalk with her suitcase. I popped the trunk and put our luggage inside. I opened the door for Mother, then ran around to the driver's side. Mother pulled the pack of cigarettes out from beneath the passenger seat. She passed one to me then pressed in the lighter with a pop of her wrist. We waved at Father as I drove away without a clue as to our destination.

THE SEA DOG INN

"Where are we headed, Mother?" I said.

"Back to the Cape, Jack," she said.

"Really? To the Honeysuckle?"

"No, not the Honeysuckle. I thought we'd go a little further up the coast this time. I found a place in North Eastham that I think will suit us just fine."

The drive was smooth, and I began to see familiar sights: the Bourne Bridge, Route 6, the maddening rotaries. I flicked my middle finger at the sign for Hyannis Port and drove straight on toward Eastham. I liked the way things felt as we rolled along with traffic. The world around us seemed slower than when we'd been on the mid-Cape in July, and I imagined this is what Mother was looking for.

"The directions say to turn left up there by the motel, Jack. Follow the winding road past the little school, then bear around the curve and park just past the flagpole," Mother said.

I repeated the directions aloud as the car bumped down the sandy beach road, until I'd made the last turn and shifted the gear into park at the only flagpole in sight. A tattered banner of the stars and stripes flapped in the breeze, reminding me of the sound of mother snapping the sheets as she folded them by the clothesline in our backyard. In front of us stood a weathered gray two-story house with white shutters. A navy blue oval sign hung over the screened in porch. Scrolled in gold letters, the sign read *The Sea Dog Inn*. The name made me smile.

"Well, this is it," Mother said, climbing out of the car and stretching her legs. She took her sunglasses off and shoved them down into her purse. "Looks just like the picture on the brochure. Just lovely!" She clasped her hands in front of her heart and glowed.

I stretched out, too, then looked around at the other Cape houses sprinkling the beach road.

111

"They're here!" someone yelled from indoors. A little girl with corkscrew curls and torn overalls rushed down from the porch.

"Hello," she said, squinting up at us.

"Why, hello there," Mother cooed.

"Hi," I said.

"Are you the Sullivans?" she said.

"We are," Mother said, smiling as she followed the young girl up to the front steps.

"Grandmother said for me to escort you inside." The girl fanned her hand toward the front door, then stooped down to tie a knot in her high-top sneakers. A herd of boys rode by on their bicycles, beach bound I assumed by the towels draped over their bare shoulders. They looked no older than her, maybe the fifth or sixth grade.

"Coming down to beach, Dani?" the one trailing in the back called out to her.

"Sure thing," she said, running over and yanking a dripping towel off of the porch ledge.

"*Danielle?*" A voice creaked out like an old set of stairs. A hand pressed against the screen door.

"Gram?" she called back.

"Be back in one hour."

"Yes, ma'am!" Danielle said, racing down the sandy road after the others.

Mother put her hand up over her eyes and peered toward the door.

"Excuse me, ma'am. We're the Sullivans. We have reservations at the Inn," Mother said.

A brown wooden cane knocked open the screen door. A hunch backed woman made her way onto the porch, smiling like she had won the lottery.

"I've been looking forward to your visit, Mrs. Sullivan. I'm Louise Simone. Welcome to the Sea Dog!"

"Oh, Claire. Please, call me Claire," Mother said, rushing up the steps to take hold of the door behind Mrs. Simone. Mother put her hand beneath her elbow and guided her out onto the porch.

"This must be the son you wrote me about. Jack?" Mrs. Simone said, waving her cane in my direction.

I walked up the stairs and rested my hand on her arm. "Pleasure to meet you, ma'am. We're looking forward to being your guests," I said.

"Well come in, let me show you to your rooms," she said, turning around in a slow circle. "That little spitfire you met on the porch was Danielle, my granddaughter. She's up visiting for the week. I sure do love visitors. Did I mention how happy I am to have you?"

"Yes, and thank you," Mother said.

I ran back to the car and grabbed our bags, running back up the stairs to catch up with Mother. My nose twitched from the smell of the place. The musty air reminded me of my grandparents' attic.

"Not sure what you're used to," said Mrs. Simone. "But be sure to let me know if you need anything to make you a bit more comfortable."

She led Mother and me into the Inn. It was dark inside; the only light was what filtered in from the windows and between the blinds. Mrs. Simone shuffled down a narrow hall lined with cherry wooden cupboard doors and used the end of her cane to give a hard smack to the first cupboard. "In here you'll find your beach towels." She rapped the next one. "And right here you'll find the bath towels, followed by the linens in cupboard number three."

Mrs. Simone walked to the very end of the dim hall and did a u-turn, then arched her shoulders further then I thought they could go, and scooted underneath the stairwell. She plunked down on a round, wooden stool covered with splotches of white chipped paint.

"This here is a relaxation spot. Thought it would be nice, especially for the city folk coming to the Sea Dog in need of some R and R." At that moment, what sounded

113

like a herd of animals bound down the stairs, sending the staircase shaking above Mrs. Simone's head. She didn't flinch. Instead, she closed her eyes and sucked in air through her pointed noise. My god, she inhaled for so long that I thought she was going to suck all the air out of the house, then she pursed her lips paper thin and blew all the air out through the slightest part.

"There now," she said reaching out for my hand, pulling herself up, and brushing past Mother and I. As we walked near the front door and rounded right up the staircase, I looked at Mother, pointed toward the car and raised my shoulders in a *should we make a run for it?* kind of way. The Sea Dog was crazier than the Honeysuckle, I thought. Mother fought back a laugh, then coughed against the back of her hand when Mrs. Simone turned around to glance at her.

Up the stairs we walked, passing by amateur paintings that covered the walls. The paintings looked kind of nice in their own way. They made me feel like if I painted something it might stand a shot at hanging on the wall and being a part of the Sea Dog legacy.

The hall was painted a dark forest green and had more of a campy feel to me than a beach one. A deer's head faced us head on and a border of loons painted in cream ran along the middle of the wall.

"My room is the last one down," Mrs. Simone said. "There are the three boarding rooms on this floor and two others in the attic. I keep the adults down here and the youngsters upstairs, if I can help it. Hate to hear all that rock-n-roll at night. Upstairs they are free to play it as loud as they want!" She turned to me with a youthful smile. "Did you bring your records, Jack?" She opened an unnamed door.

"No, ma'am. I left my records at home," I said.

"Well, downstairs in the living room there's a whole stack. Feel free to borrow whichever ones you'd like and bring them up to your room."

"Thank you, ma'am." I could feel trickles of sweat drip down my back. The place was stifling.

"Now this here is your room, Claire. Quite simple, that's our way," Mrs. Simone said.

I brought Mother's bag in and laid it on the end of her bed. The room was the barest room I had ever seen. A single wrought iron bed was pushed under a small window. A yellow and white checkered quilt covered it. A chair was angled in the corner, electric blue fabric, with a white enamel wash bowl and a faded towel on it. Against the wall was a short dresser with a rectangular mirror hanging above it. Some old country hat with big, fake flowers sticking out of it hung off the mirror's edge. Against the other wall were a few wooden crates, stocked high with tattered paperbacks.

"It's perfect," Mother said, flopping down on her bed with a sigh. "Just perfect." She was giddy, Mother was, and I couldn't figure out why. Beside the fact that she seemed to be melting into the quilt with a smile covering her face, this wasn't the type of room she was used to staying in. I couldn't have cared either way, but it struck me as funny that Mother seemed so happy here in this strange mismatched space.

"I'll show Jack to his room then," Mrs. Simone said. "Oh, and remember, we're a cooperative Inn. I know I explained that to you in my letter, Mrs. Sullivan, so I'm assuming you're fine with that."

"Oh, yes, absolutely," Mother said. "When will you need us downstairs?"

"Well, it's beachcombing time now. Look there out your window," Mrs. Simone said, pointing her cane toward the foggy glass.

Mother and I pressed our temples against one another and tried to catch a glimpse of the beach through the cloudy glass. Mrs. Simone was right; it was time for the beach. Beyond the tall grass, looking past the downward slope of the dunes, Mother's room had a perfect ocean view.

"You're on the bayside," Mrs. Simone said. "You won't find a place in the world like the Cape Cod Bay. The tide is out now, perfect time for a nice walk after a long drive. Refresh your senses."

"Beautiful," Mother said.

"Well then, if you meet me in the kitchen at a half-past four that should do the trick. Dinner's on at six. Dessert on the porch at seven. Games at eight for anyone interested, and lights out at ten. I lock the doors by ten-thirty, so if you're not indoors, then you'll be camping out on the beach. Sleeping bags are in the shed!" she laughed.

Mother turned toward me. "There's no Maybelle in these parts, Jack. We're expected to cook our meals together; all the guests will do their share," Mother said, nodding at me. "So you'll be expected in the kitchen when Mrs. Simone tells you."

All of a sudden, I was feeling the need for a little breathing room. Running off back to the Cape was fine by me, but it still didn't take away the fact that my family was falling apart.

"Ok," I said with a shrug. "I'll see you later then, Mother."

"C'mon, Jack! Let's get you settled," Mrs. Simone said.

Mrs. Simone's voice rattled like an old window during a storm, though it didn't make you feel on edge or anything. I kind of liked the way it sounded, real neat and all, like an old New Englander type. She seemed a little eccentric, but hell, I'd take her over Ms. Gardenia any day of the week.

"Mrs. Simone, you don't have to walk me upstairs. You can just tell me which door is mine," I said as she clutched the wobbly rail and planted one foot on the first step of the narrow, circular staircase that led to the attic.

"You're sure, Jack? It's no trouble for me," she said.

"I'm sure."

"Well then, there are just the two rooms upstairs. Your room is the first door. Letter A. Should be easy to find."

"Thank you, Mrs. Simone. I'll see you in a little while."

"4:30 in the kitchen, Jack. There's a good size crew for dinner tonight. We'll need your helping hands for sure!"

My stomach dropped since I wasn't much of a cook. "Yes, Mrs. Simone. 4:30 it is."

I headed up stairs, ducking my head so as not to whack it on the low overhead. My feet were too big for the short steps and I had to turn them sideways just to keep from falling backward. When I reached the top, I gasped for air, but it didn't seem like there was much of that. Beads of sweat broke out in a trail across my brow. I let my duffel bag slide off my shoulder, then reached my hand up underneath my shirt and swiped my back. My skin was slippery slick with sweat.

The first door had an orange letter A painted on it. Hell of a lot better than being stuck in a room named *Lilly of the Valley* like at the Honeysuckle. I pushed back the door to find a svelte brunette lying on her stomach in a white bikini. Her legs were crossed at the ankles, bobbing back and forth while she flipped through some glossy magazine.

"Sorry," I said, stumbling backward over my bag as I tried to grasp the door handle and yank it shut. Instead, my right foot twisted over the duffle bag strap, sending my left foot out in front of me. I fell forward on one knee, then hobbled around for a moment before falling sideways into the bed.

My face burned like fire. I stared down at the ground, then hopped off the bed, waving my hand back and forth at her. "Sorry, sorry. Real sorry about the intrusion. I was told this was my room. Must have been a mix up. I'll just check downstairs," I said, never once making eye contact.

"You're Jack, aren't you?" she said.

I raised my eyes to see her body bending upward then back as she sat down on her heels.

"Yes, I'm Jack," I said, eyeing her for a moment and wondering if she was someone I had met before or someone I was supposed to have known.

"Mrs. Simone tells us the guests' names before they arrive," she said, stretching her arm out to shake my hand. I pulled myself up straight as an arrow, then bent slightly at the waist and returned her handshake.

"I'm Maret," she said, "and you're right, this is your room. I just kind of took it over because I've been here all summer, and it was closest to the stairs, and frankly, I've

117

been scared out my mind sleeping up here in the attic alone each night. It's a little creepy sleeping up here by yourself."

"I can imagine. And by all means, stay here in this room. That's not a problem. I'll just take over the B room." I kicked my bag through the door and waved goodbye. "Nice to meet you, Maret."

"Yep, nice to meet you too, Jack," she said. I glanced at her again as I closed the door, just as she rolled over on her back, picked up her magazine, and rested her legs up against the wall.

I gave the second door a slight kick and it screeched open. The room was the same size as Maret's room, about the dimensions of a small walk-in closet at best. The black metal frame bed just fit the cramped space, and when I pushed the door all the way open it scraped against the foot of the bed. Underneath the window, even smaller than the one in Mother's room, was a two-shelved dresser with an old fan sitting on top of it. I yanked the dresser away from the wall and squeezed my arm in between the narrow space to plug in the cord. The speed picked up after a dozen turns, spitting out a thick layer of dust as it whirled about. I gave a couple hard coughs, then cranked the window to let in some fresh air. It must have been a long time since anyone else had tried to open the damn thing. I tried to open the window that seemed to be sealed shut and I prayed that Maret didn't hear me moaning and groaning through the walls like a big wimp. Across from my bed an old record player lay on the floor. That was it. That was all that was in the room. There wasn't a spec of anything more except a pestering mosquito and the dank smell of the olive colored sheets that felt damp to the touch.

I laid back on the bed and closed my eyes. A loud rap sounded against the wall.

"Yes?" I said.

"Hey, Jack? It's me, Maret," she said.

I was surprised at how thin the walls were. "Um, yeah. I kind of figured." I turned onto my side to face the wall that separated our rooms.

"Jack, you want me to show you the beach? I was just going down to the water myself."

I smiled, then rolled off the bed, walked out the door, and poked my head inside her room. She was still lying on her back with her feet up against the wall, twirling her wavy black hair the way I imagined a girl might twirl her finger around a phone cord when she was talking for a long time or something.

"Maret?" I said

"Oh, hey, Jack!" she said as if she wasn't expecting me. She rolled over and sprang back on her heels again.

"So do you want to go to the beach?" I said.

"Sure thing, Jack!" Her voice was light and breezy. She threw on a faded blue NYU t-shirt over her bikini, hopped into some frayed cut-off jean shorts, and slid her tanned bare feet into a pair of white leather sandals. She galloped like a horse down the stairs in front of me, while I held onto the wall for dear life. She flung out the front door, spreading her arms wide open like she had crossed the finish line first at Saratoga. She twirled around and smiled. "I've been waiting for you to get here, you know," she said.

"You have?" I said, wondering how long she had known I was coming, seeing as I just learned the news a day ago.

"Sure I have," she said steering herself around a pricker bush and holding the branches aside while I bowed away from them. "I've been waiting for you ever since your mom wrote her letter to Mrs. Simone."

"When was that? The letter?"

"Oh, I don't know, maybe two weeks ago. Could have been three."

It struck me that three weeks ago was further back then the night I had walked in on Father. There must have been other things he'd done that that I didn't know about. That last night at the Honeysuckle must have been the last straw.

Maret pointed ahead to the sandy path that led to a set of wooden stairs. I followed her down the steps. Massive rocks jutted out on each side of us. Maret jumped from the third step. Her feet sank into a hole in the sand. I followed her, jumping down, then kicking my shoes off underneath the stairs.

119

"Want to walk down the beach or out toward the sea? The tide is pretty far out, looks like we could walk a good mile," she said, pulling the NYU shirt off and leaving it in a heap on top of my shoes.

"Out to sea," I said, wincing as I remembered how only a week ago, I'd wanted to run out to sea and never come back. "On second thought, let's just head down the beach."

Maret kicked sand when she walked, spraying it all over. The wind carried it sideways into my face. I didn't mind. She seemed kind of clueless about it, which I thought was sort of cute. Though cute wasn't the word I would really use to describe Maret. She was a knockout.

"Do you go to NYU?" I said, staring straight ahead, feeling a little too awkward to make eye contact with her.

"I do," she said, pulling her hair back into some sort of twisted knot and piercing a long stick down through it that she had found along the shore. "Going into my sophomore year. Still have to figure my major out." She stuffed her hands deep in the pockets of her cut-off jean shorts. "Not sure yet what it'll be. What about you?"

"Going into my Senior year in high school. Hoping to go to Harvard after that." I tilted my head and scratched the back of my neck. Maret didn't say a word about Harvard. She kept on talking about the Cape. Harvard didn't seem to faze her.

"I'd always wanted to work on the Cape for a summer. I saw an ad last year when I came on vacation with my parents. It was late August, so I gave Mrs. Simone a call. She invited me over for tea, and now I'm sort of the housekeeper of the place. It's an easy gig. Comes with free housing, meals and a little money each week. What I'm really trying to do is write some good songs while I'm out here though. There's a lot of quiet time to do that. I met some people back in New York who know some people in the music business. I'm hoping to leave here with some good material come September. What about you?"

"What do you mean?"

"What do you mean, what do I mean?" she laughed and gave me a playful push toward the water. "What are your interests? What kinds of things do you like to do? What makes you tick?"

"Hmm, well, I guess I'm good at sports. But to be honest, they're kind of starting to bore me."

"Well, that's a start. So what do you do for fun?"

"Um, I like the beach, you know, swimming, hanging out."

"And?"

"And what? I don't know. What am I supposed to like? I'm in high school." I laughed, though I was feeling a little pressured to tell her who I was. Hell, I didn't even know that much.

"*Jack, Jack, Jack.* I'm leaving in two weeks to go back to New York. Is that all the time I have you for?" she said, reaching up and rustling my hair.

"Yep, something like that." I breathed in so much air that I felt my chest balloon up. I looked over at her. She was shaking her head and smiling, a real pretty smile. Her skin wasn't just tan, it was golden brown. Her eyes were green as emeralds, and had little glints of brown in them. Small turquoise earrings swung from her ears.

I blew out all the air that I was holding in. I laughed one of those nervous laughs, even though I was finally feeling relaxed around her. I felt myself smiling too, right along with her, so I bit my lip real hard. She probably thought I looked miserable the way I'd clamped right down on it and cut off my smile. But I had to, I was afraid that if I didn't keep ahold of it, I would break into one of those real goofy grins. You know, a grin like the one when I was a kid and Bitty O'Toole, one of the older girls in the neighborhood, rode by the front yard on her bicycle. I'm not sure why they called her Bitty, because as she sped down the sidewalk in her stretchy pink top, I'd known right then that Bitty was anything but. Her white tennis skirt kind of flew up a little bit on the side, not a lot, not enough where I actually saw anything, but just enough, just enough for me to go and get that dopey look on my face and have Thomas smack my head and call me some crushing name over it in front of whomever else was around.

Maret started talking, snapping me back to reality. I loosened the hold of my lip, and switched to my nervous chew on the inside of my cheek. I guess I wasn't as relaxed around her as I'd thought, or hoped.

"Well, two weeks is not a lot of time, Jack." She walked closer to the ocean and dipped her feet in the white foam. "Looks like I've got a lot of work to do!"

"What do you mean by that?" I said, digging my heel in the sand, never thinking of myself as someone's project.

She pushed a loose strand of her hair back and held it behind her ear so the wind didn't catch hold of it again. I counted the brown freckles on her nose. There were seven all together, three on each side and one smack dab in the middle of the bridge. "The Sea Dog is a place people come when they're a little lost. Didn't you know, Jack?"

"Who said I was lost?" I creased my eyes at her.

"Nobody. I figured it was your mother who was lost." Maret held on tight to that wisp of hair that kept flying out in front of her face.

"Yeah, you're right about that. I'm just along for the ride," I said.

"Well, whether you're here for you or just tagging along with her, one thing's for sure."

"What's that?"

"Everybody leaves the Sea Dog feeling like they've found something."

"Well, then, maybe I will too."

I turned and looked down the beach in the direction of where we'd begun our walk. I stuffed my hands deeper into my pocket and squinted at the shore. We walked in quiet back to the Sea Dog. The winds rolled in off the ocean, whipping past us. I heard the whispers of sweet Isabelle in my ear, and for the first time all week, the death grip around my throat released itself. And I breathed.

122

FAMILY STYLE

"It's called family style, Jack, and you'll love it!" Mrs. Simone said as she banged her cane along the kitchen floor boards and shuffled over to the refrigerator. She jostled the crisper drawer, then rolled three red bell peppers down the counter at me.

I stood facing the kitchen counter. My hand was clenched around a butter knife. What the hell was I supposed to do with the peppers? I thought as they slowed to a stop in front of my face. I kept staring at those peppers until I'd imagined they'd sprouted little feet, and each had little versions of Mrs. Simone's cane. I pictured them hustling across the counter and escaping back to the refrigerator. I stared and stared, until I heard Maret waltz in singing *hello!* before giving Mrs. Simone a gentle hug.

Maret wore a loose red smock top that looked like a bandana from an old Western film. She sprung up onto the counter next. A piece of frayed denim from her jean shorts grazed my forearm. "The peppers are for the salad, Jack. You just have to chop 'em up into thin slices." She leaned past me to pull a wooden cutting board down from the cupboard. She flipped it over on the counter like a flap jack, then hopped down, wrenched open a wedged drawer, pulled out a shorter, sharper knife, and placed it in my hand.

"Salad?" I said

"Salad," Maret said.

I nodded. "I can do salad."

"Mr. and Mrs. Willmot?" Mrs. Simone called out to the porch where a Canadian couple sat playing checkers. "You're in charge of lighting the coals on the grill. I have tuna steaks in the fridge. You know the drill!"

"I'm here!" Mother said, springing through the doorway looking nothing at all like the mother I knew. Her shoulders were loose and relaxed. Her face glowed from the sun. Why it seemed like little specs of golden sunlight had just fallen all over her the way she stood there glowing like that. Her hair was wet and curly; she hadn't bothered to dry or style it. She wore a long, cotton dress and I could see her bathing suit straps underneath.

I'd never seen Mother come to dinner in anything but a proper evening dress. Hell, even on nights when the heat was scorching, and Thomas, Father, and I sat around in our boxer shorts, Mother was always dressed to the nines. But what struck me most was that she was barefoot.

"Claire! Claire, I'm so happy to see you!" Mrs. Simone said, wrapping her arms around my mother in a giant bear hug, her cane still in her hand. Mother's eyes closed and I noticed how she sunk into Mrs. Simone. Even mothers needs to be hugged, I thought.

"Claire, I need you to do the garlic bread, then please set the table. The Morgan couple will be dining out with family in Chatam tonight. Poor pair, they've been trying to conceive for five years now, can you believe it? Let's hope the old Sea Dog magic does its trick, yes?"

"Yes!" the women in the kitchen cried out.

Sweat beaded on my forehead and I focused on slicing the peppers the way Maret had told me to. I kind of couldn't believe that Mrs. Simone was talking about people getting lucky while my own mother stood less than five feet from me. Just focus on the peppers, I told myself. Focus on the peppers. Don't look around, just stare at the knife. Finally, the conversation switched gears and thank God for that because there was nothing left for me to slice up or chop.

I walked into the dining room and noticed the different colored place settings on the table. It was nothing like the white china I was used to. Nope, there were blue plates, and green bowls, and all sizes of drinking glasses that were shades of purple.

"We're an eclectic bunch," Maret said with a wink.

I smiled and shrugged my shoulders. It seemed like people felt they had to explain their differences to me. I guess they didn't see me as being one in the same.

At the Honeysuckle, the camaraderie had been superficial. But here at the Sea Dog, I felt a sense of peace with the strangers around me in a matter of minutes. Everyone grabbed the nearest seat. We all grabbed a dish or platter and served up food onto one another's plates when someone asked. We passed things down the table the way real families do in their own kitchens. We shared funny stories and everyone laughed full belly laughs, and it all felt so real and so goddamn good. I looked up at the clock and was disappointed that the dinner hour was ending.

"Don't forget, dessert on the porch," Mrs. Simone sang out. "Maret's made a lemon meringue pie!"

"How heavenly!" Mother said.

"What an angel," I whispered under my breath.

"I heard that, Jack," Maret said, clicking her tongue and raising her eyebrows at me as I smirked and headed out to the porch.

That night, after our lemon meringue pie, and a ridiculous round of charades, I retired to my room in the attic. Maret was in charge of clean up. I asked her if I might help, but she insisted not.

"This is what I get paid the big bucks for," she said with a wink.

I laughed and took in a huge breath. What's with all this deep breathing, I wondered.

I rounded the corner on the second floor and popped my head into Mother's room to say goodnight. She sat sideways in a reading chair. Her feet dangled over the arm. A pair of knitting needles and a ball of yarn lay in her lap. Her eyes were closed, so I walked over, moved the needle and yarn to the side table, and covered her with a blanket. I dimmed the light and whispered good night before shutting the door. She looked the picture of paradise, my Mother did. The Sea Dog Inn, I laughed to myself, who would have thought that this was where she'd find her solace?

I turned to find Mrs. Simone closing the curtains at the end of the hall. "Breakfast is at eight in the morning, Jack," she said.

"Thank you, Mrs. Simone. Good night." I waved down the hall at her. Part of me wanted to walk down the hall and give the old woman a hug, but I refrained.

Upstairs, I lay on my bed and took out my notepad and the washed out, crumbling piece of paper with Isabelle's address on it. I'd read her address over so many times, studying her street name, Picador Lane, her town name, Charleston, South Carolina, and now here I was staring at it again, picturing sweet Izzy in her childhood bed and wishing I was there with her. I put my hands behind my head and rested back on the lumpy pillow.

Izzy must've arrived home from the Honeysuckle by now, I thought. I could picture her there, tucked away under her covers, only weeks away from starting her Senior year, too. I had to write to her soon so she'd have my address here at the Sea Dog. I lay on my side, smoking a cigarette, and writing to Izzy all about the journey back to the Cape, how Mother seemed happier, how we were staying at this unusual place for the next three weeks, and how it seemed there had been a plan to come here for quite some time.

I hoped to make Izzy laugh when I wrote to her about our initial tour of the Sea Dog, then frowned to think I wouldn't be able to hear any of her reactions. As I signed off my name and held the paper against my bare chest, I stared off into space, remembering Izzy's smile and her featherlike touch. I turned off my light and lay there, twisting my head back, and staring out the little square window, praying I'd see a shooting star flash by so I could get myself a free wish.

I rolled over onto my back. I was feeling hot, sleepless, restless. I wanted to escape for a walk, but then remembered Mrs. Simone's words, *The Inn gets locked up at ten, after that you're camping out on the beach*, and all at once, I felt trapped. I turned toward the wall and decided to give a couple raps against it. For whatever reason, I couldn't quite tell you.

There were two raps back. Maret was awake. I laid there frozen, petrified like. What if she thought I was some creep who wanted to see her in her pajamas? Ah shit, I always felt like I was screwing things up, looking like a weirdo or something.

She rapped twice again. I rapped once back. The next rap came at my door.

"You awake in there, Jack?" she said.

I reached over and turned on the light as she pushed open the door.

"Maret, sorry if I woke you. I couldn't sleep. I thought maybe you'd be in the same boat," I said, sitting up in bed.

She wore black spectacle glasses and an oversized white cotton nightgown, which surprised me. She looked kind of nerdy all of a sudden, nothing like the sophisticated bombshell that I'd seen lying across the bed in her white bikini.

"Come with me, there's a fire escape at the end of the hall. We can sit outside there and cool down a bit," she said.

I trailed after her, crawling outside behind her onto the iron ledge. She pulled her nightgown up over her head and hung it over the ledge. "Man, it's hot out tonight," she said, fanning her face.

My breath became trapped in my chest and my body froze. I was scared to look over and find her completely naked or something, but when I did look over I breathed a quiet sigh because she still had on a camisole and pair of cotton shorts. We sat down and leaned our upper bodies forward, crossing our arms over the black metal bar in front of us. We swung our feet in the air the way little kids do when they can't touch the ground.

Maret rested her head on her forearms and closed her eyes. I stared around at the nothingness of the night, feeling a little uncomfortable being out there alone with her like that.

"You made a real nice salad tonight, Jack." Her chin was pressed into her forearms.

"Thank you, Maret."

"Are you always so polite?"

"I try."

"That's a nice quality about you, Jack."

"Thank you, Maret."

"So what's keeping you up late at night? Can't just be the heat." She laid her cheek where her chin had been and gazed at me.

"Nothing much, just so damn muggy in that room," I said.

"It's ok, Jack. You can tell me what it is," she said.

"Nah." Now I was the one pressing my chin into my arm. Ah shit, I thought, because I really did feel like telling her everything for some reason.

"I'm a real good listener, Jack."

"You promise you're not going to write it into a song?" I was half joking, half serious.

She pulled her legs up and scooted them underneath her bottom. She reached out for my hand. I laid my cheek to my forearm and let my left arm go limp and fall out toward her. She took hold of it, and just held it there in between her two hands. I lifted my eyes up to hers, and there she was staring back me as if I was the only person in the world that mattered.

"I promise, Jack."

And so I told her everything I could think to tell her about my mother and father, inserting any memory I had that I thought might make sense out of the crazy turn our family had taken. I choked up a little here and there, and she just held my hand and kept looking at me as if to say, *I'm still listening, so don't stop talking*. It felt good to tell my story to someone, especially to someone who was in no way connected to the Honeysuckle Inn. Because as much as I loved my Izzy, I had begun to loathe every memory I had of the Honeysuckle; lately, I'd found myself wishing that I could erase the damn place from my mind altogether.

When there was nothing left to say, I peeked at Maret from the corner of my eye to see what she was doing. She had stopped looking at me, which was kind of nice. It's like she knew the story had come to an end. She stared at my hands. She rubbed her fingertips up and down each of my fingers, going up and over each of my fingernails. She took hold of my hands, kissed each one at the center of my palm, then pressed them together. She scooted up really close to me as she pressed my hands to her heart.

"You're a really strong person, Jack. You're going to get through all of this and come out shining." She stared right at me, straight into my eyes.

"You think?" I said.

"I know," she said.

My face flushed and heat rose to my cheeks. I was glad it was too dark for her to see.

"I'm happy you're here at the Sea Dog, Jack. I think that you and I were meant to cross paths."

"Me too, Maret."

She suspended her arms over the rail and sunk her chin into her crossed wrists. We stayed out on the fire escape for hours longer, just sitting still and staring out at the darkness. And then the night turned to dusk and soft ginger hues began filling up the sky.

"I'm feeling kind of beat, Maret," I said, looking over at her with a meek smile. "I'm sorry I've kept you out here so long. I forgot that you have to work this morning."

"It was my idea," she said, yawning like lion.

I stood and pulled her up. I pulled her nightgown off the ledge and she moved my hands so that they were holding the top part open as she pushed her head through, and then her arms.   "Thank you," she whispered.

Then I braced the window so she could crawl through. She waved goodnight, stumbled down the hall, and fell sideways into her room.

In my room, I pressed my face down against the clock on the floor to read it. 3:43 a.m. I crashed back onto my bed, sleep finally having set in. I rapped twice on the wall, Maret rapped back, and I fell asleep.

*****

I woke to the slow creak of my door and the sunlight blaring through the square window. I leaned up in bed, pressed my hands against my eyes, then squinted and watched as Maret walked toward my dresser with a green wicker tray. I yanked the sheet up over my pinstripe boxers, rubbed my eyes, and stared at the tray in wonder.

"You slept through breakfast," she said, bright-eyed and cheery.

"Thanks, Maret," I said, looking over at a blueberry muffin, sprinkled with sugar, and a tall glass of orange juice with specs of pulp around the rim of the glass. She walked backward out of the room, fluttered her fingers at me, and shut the door.

I took a bite of the muffin, rested my head back against my pillow, and chewed with my eyes closed. The next person to come through the door was Mother.

"Jack? Jack?" she said. "Why are you in bed at this hour? Are you feeling ok?"

129

"What time is it?" I said, rubbing my eyes harder this time, sitting up and brushing the muffin crumbs off my chest.

"It's nearly noon, Jack. You're expected to help with lunch! People are going to be at the table any minute. Have you been asleep all day?" She unzipped my duffel bag and pulled out a set of clothes, then laid them across the foot of my bed.

"I didn't fall asleep until real late, Mother. Give me five minutes. I'll be right down."

I threw on my shorts and t-shirt. I spit on my fingers and tapped at the front of my hair, feeling my damn cowlick standing and flopping with each step I took. Ah, forget it, I thought as I hustled down to the kitchen, afraid of being late or letting anyone down.

"Mr. Sullivan!" Mrs. Simone said. "Please set the table. You'll be in charge of scooping out ice-cream once we've finished lunch. We need your strong muscles for that I'm sure!"

Set the table, I thought. I could handle setting the table.

It felt good to help. Lunch was bacon, lettuce and tomato sandwiches, simple and delicious. We ate on the porch, and when everyone had finished, I served up bowl after bowl of vanilla ice-cream. We all laughed through each spoonful. Maret came in with her guitar and played us some songs she'd written. Mother excused herself to the car and came back with a handful of photos. She asked if the others might like to see them. And they did like seeing them, too. In fact, they loved seeing them, and they all told her so.

I looked around on this second day at the Sea Dog and smiled in disbelief. Strange, I thought, thinking back to the quiet of our family meals where no one spoke, but instead rushed through every bite to get the damn occasion of dinner over with. Poor Mother would have prepared and cleaned up everything by herself. No wonder she loved it here at the Sea Dog. It felt so much better to me to be a real part of something then to be alone. I decided that family style was a style I quite liked, and a style I was surprised to find in a room with Mother and a bunch of strangers.

SNAPSHOTS

Mother had spent the past few weeks forming new habits. In the morning, I'd look out my window and see her silhouette walking the beach. I knew it was her by the floppy straw hat she wore. After lunch she'd say she was going for a drive, though she didn't really *say* it; she kind of sang it. *Going for a drive!* and then there would be the pitter-patter of her middle-aged feet as she ran down the front hall and let the screen door crash behind her.

"What do you do on your drives, Mother?" I asked her one night as we swung on the lopsided wooden porch swing.

"It's the most wonderful time, Jack. I drive about, get myself good and lost, and I take pictures. Loads of them. You should come with me sometime. Would you like that?" Her eyes arched like a rainbow.

"Of course. I'd love to go with you sometime."

"I always snap the same thing, though. You might find yourself bored!"

"What is it?"

"Houses. My photos are mostly of houses."

"Houses. Ah, I remember."

"Do you?" She turned toward me. "Do you remember, Jack?"

"Sure I do. You always seemed to be taking photos of houses. What was the fascination?"

"No fascination, really. I suppose I just liked them."

"Well, there had to be some reason," I said, pressing her on as I'd learned how to do from my talks with Maret.

Mother reached under the green cotton bench cushion and pulled out a pack of cigarettes. It was the first time I'd seen her smoke since we'd arrived at the Sea Dog. She inhaled a long, slow drag, then stretched her legs out in front of her, resting them on the water-stained coffee table.

131

"When I was at Vassar, I used to walk around the neighborhoods and peek into the different houses. I'd think about all that might be happening inside of those homes. Might sound a little odd to you, I know. But it was kind of fun to do. I'd try to steal a glimpse of a family eating dinner, kids doing homework around the table, old men reading the evening paper in a chair, flowers pouring out of flowerboxes in spring, dog leashes hanging from a porch swing in summer, bicycles scattered across front lawns like back when you and Thomas were real little, that sort of thing. I suppose it has become a fascination of mine, capturing all of those different houses."

As she spoke, I could picture her on one of her outings, pulling over the car and rolling down the window to snap a white colonial with black shutters.

"I used to daydream about the different lives I would lead living in each of those houses. Not that I wasn't happiest with you, Jack. Understand that. I was just always so curious about the many paths that people travel in life."

"I understand, Mother. How long have you've been taking photos of houses then?"

"Oh, let's see, it would be a little over twenty years now. The photos are all stuffed away in boxes. I never really did anything with them, just liked taking the shots."

She stood up and walked over to the porch door, opening it and flicking her cigarette butt outdoors. She turned back toward me and pulled the sides of her blue cardigan across the front of her.

"Brr. Such a cool breeze. Are you cold, Jack?"

"No, Mother. I'm fine."

She came over and kissed the top of my head. "Sweet dreams, my darling boy."

"Goodnight, Mother."

I listened to her walk indoors and up the stairs one at a time as I pulled out a smoke from her secret stash under the cushion, struck a light, and walked outside. I moseyed around the front lawn, tilting my head back and looking up at the stars.

For over twenty years, my mother had told herself that she was merely taking a few pictures, trying to capture some nice shots of houses. When really, for over twenty years, my mother had been trying to distinguish the meaning of those houses. All of those beautiful houses, and she was trying to imagine what made them a *home*, trying to imagine herself in the throes. I guess our house in Ithaca didn't feel any better to her than it had to me all these years. But how could it when your heart just wasn't there?

A memory floated across my mind. I was young, three, maybe four. We'd dropped Thomas off at school, then walked the sidewalk into town. Mother had me pose by a tire swing dangling from a big Oak tree. I didn't like the tire swing, hadn't stopped to see it on my own. I wonder now if she'd been trying to take a picture of the house behind me. I was curious to find that picture, find that house, and see what all the fuss had been about.

It was a nice surprise to me when I discovered that Mother had been sharing her photos with her new friends come family here at the Sea Dog.

"They're gorgeous, Jack. Have you seen them?" Maret said as she poked her head into my room to say goodnight after washing the dinner dishes. I was doing sit-ups and came up to my knees to pull on my t-shirt.

"I saw them awhile back. I remember her taking the shots when I was little. She has a way with the camera, that's for sure." I said, wiping the sweat off my forehead with the back of my hand.

Maret traipsed in and sat on my bed, right up near my pillow. I could see my reflection in the window, and tried to tap down the front pieces of hair that were sticking up all over the place. I put my back against the wall and slid down to the ground, propping my feet up on the mattress and crossing them at the ankles.

Maret wore a short white robe. Her hair was pulled back with a terry cloth band. I could see the tan line around her forehead. She curled her feet up underneath her bottom. She seemed awful comfortable just popping over in her pajamas. It must have been a college thing, I thought. She raised her shoulders real high and let them down slowly as she spoke. "Your mother has folders full of her pictures. It's amazing. I told her she should really put together a portfolio," she said.

"I'm glad you're so interested in them. It must make her feel good to have someone so interested," I said.

"It's nice when people are interested in the things you love to do," she said, laying back and stretching her legs out. The tips of our toes touched. I noticed the little silver ring on her fourth toe.

"Which reminds me," she said, turning on her side and pressing her cheek against my pillow. "Your interests?" Her golden face looked so fresh and clean against the crisp white pillow case. And her lips were a rosy red.

"Oh yeah, how could I forget," I laughed, and tilted my head back against the wall.

"Well, I like doing stuff in the kitchen. That may sound funny, but it's kind of neat to help make stuff, you know, help out with things."

"I'm glad you think so, Jack. And it's also about being together, isn't it?"

"It is. And it's nice being around people who laugh. That's a real change for Mother and me."

"Don't you laugh much, Jack?" She seemed concerned. She sat up, then slid off the bed and onto the floor. She pressed her back against the bed frame and pulled her knees up high. I tried not to stare at the purple satin underwear hugging her bottom and peeking out from underneath her robe.

I cleared my throat. "I laugh. Yeah, sure I laugh."

"I think you're lying. I don't think that you laugh too much at all."

"I laugh, believe me. I laugh."

"Tell me the best laughs you've had." She sat up on her feet and leaned forward waiting for my answer.

I scratched my head thinking real hard about it. Goddamit, I really couldn't remember too many times.

"That's ok, Jack." She scooted over to my side of the wall and stretched her legs out again. "Maybe there hasn't been too much to laugh about?"

"Nope, I guess not." I chewed my nails up a bit. "But I like to laugh, you know. I like to laugh a whole lot."

"That's wonderful, Jack." She reached down for my hand and placed hers over top of mine.

*****

We found our way to each other on most nights. We'd meet up in one of our rooms, on the fire escape, or down in the screened in porch. I began to see Maret as a therapist type. She helped me open up about stuff I didn't know was all closed up to begin with. She had a way of asking me just the right questions and on I'd go talking about all the things I'd never really talked about with anyone, things like Father and Thomas, and seeing Mother so unhappy, and what if I did get into Harvard and actually went to the damn place. And then I told her all about my loving Izzy, and my feeling guilty because after I'd written her that I was at the Sea Dog, she did write back, twice in one week alone, and for some reason I kept trailing off mid-sentence in my response to her and never finished any of my letters, nor mailed another one out after the single one I'd written her on my first night there. And I even spilled the beans about having sex a few weeks back for the first time, and what a failure I'd been at that, and how badly I wanted to have sex again and get it right. And all the while, all the nights that I talked and talked, Maret listened and asked me more questions in this delicate way which made me want to tell her things I hadn't thought about in years. By the end of the second week, I thought there wasn't anything left I could tell her.

"Why did you want to know all about me?" I said one night as I lay across her bed.

"Why did you want to tell me?" she said.

"Is that a trick question, Maret?"

"No, and I don't want you to give me some trick answer." She studied my face.

135

"I wanted to tell you because it felt safe to tell you, because the more I told you the more I wanted you to know. Because if you knew everything and still thought I was ordinary and not some messed up kid, then maybe there'd be a chance that no matter what happens between my Mother and Father, I'd still have a shot at turning out like a regular guy, which would seem pretty difficult when you consider the gene pool of pricks that I come from. And because you're nice, and you listen, and when I catch you writing your songs on the beach I find myself a little bit curious about you," I said. I was sitting up now, leaning my forearms over my knees, chewing my nails so hard that they stung. "And that wasn't a trick answer, Maret. That was me just telling you the truth."

"Good night, Jack," she said, her eyes brimming with tears.

"I'm sorry if I upset you, Maret," I said. "I'm sorry, really, I am." I fumbled my way out of her room.

I went into my room and fell back down on my bed. I felt my stomach twist itself into a tight knot. It was tough being in a room so close to her, and hard not to feel trapped at times like this. I wasn't sure why she'd gotten all teary, and my nerves were shot lying there worrying about what I'd said to upset her. I heard a rap on the wall. I rapped back. Then there was a rap on my door and Maret let herself in.

"Back there in my room," she said, curling herself up at the bottom of my bed. "You sounded like, well, like you might be feeling about me things that I can't let myself feel about you."

I bit my lip and shook my head. "You've changed me, Maret. That's all. I'm just grateful for you." My insides screamed out something different. This older girl, who'd listened to me and kind of cared for me like a lost puppy, hell, she'd made things better. She had. And for that I kind of loved her. But I knew she was older, two years at that. She was in college. I was in high school. She wasn't interested in someone like me.

"Oh, Jack," she said. "You're going to turn heads someday. Wait until you get to college. College girls will fall head over heels for a young man like you."

I knew she was trying to wash the salt out of my wounds, but I just wanted her to leave. I didn't want to wait until I got to college to turn the heads of city girls like Maret; I wanted to turn them now.

"Good night, Jack," she said, and slipped out of my room. She rapped once more on the wall that night. The sound made me feel like I was going to puke, so I tucked my hands up under my pillow, and promised myself I'd finish Izzy's letter and mail it first thing in the morning, then I fell asleep.

*****

The next night after chili dogs and crinkle cut fries, and sugar cookies for dessert, I lay in bed an anxious mess. I was unable to sleep, though unable to move from my bed and leave my room either. There was no rap on the wall, and I didn't dare rap either, even after I'd heard the second floor shower blasting, Maret tip-toeing up the stairs, and the thud of her body against the squeaky metal bed in her room.

I turned toward the wall and touched it with my fingertips. I pretended to knock on it, did so lightly even. My heart ached for her. It ached to tell her more about me, to free all of those burdens, to get around to asking her more about herself, even though she never seemed too interested in sharing with me as much as she seemed interested in listening to me.

Just as my eyelids grew heavy and my body loose, I heard the creak of my door. The moonlight poured in through the little square window and when I looked up from my bed, I saw Maret standing there.

"Are you awake, Jack?" she said.

"Hi, Maret," I said.

"Jack, after all you told me, I want you to know that I *do* think you are completely normal, and that you *are* different from what I imagine your father and brother to be, and that beyond normal, you're an *extraordinary* person, Jack. You *really* are. And I'm sorry that things feel weird between us." She curled up on the bottom of my bed, her feet tucked underneath her. "I'm sorry for not having been able to hear everything you had to

137

say, as much I wanted to. I guess in the way that there were some things you didn't know you were ready to talk about, there were some things I wasn't ready to hear."

"I understand, Maret." Though I didn't know what I really understood at all. I wanted to spew out every reason why I liked her, every reason why I thought she should like me, or at least try to anyway. After all, someday I *would* be in college. I'd be a freshman when she'd be a senior, so what excuse would she have then? But I didn't have to talk, because now it was my turn to listen.

"You know tomorrow's my last day working here, right Jack?" she said.

"I remember," I said. "You've got to go back to New York. Back to college."

"I do."

"You said we'd all leave the Sea Dog finding something, didn't you?" I was leaning up now, resting my arms on my knees, biting down on my bottom lip, and taking a good, hard look at her through the dark.

"I sure did," she said. "What do you think you've found, Jack?"

"I don't know. I guess learning how to get through those bad times that life throws at you. I don't have a clue what's waiting for me or Mother back home, but I know she's found herself in her photography again. And I've found out that it's possible to talk about what's chewing at my mind, thanks to you, Maret. It's been a great visit here. It truly has."

"You know I meant what I said last night, as much as you probably didn't want to hear it. You'll find someone, Jack."

"But it won't be you," I teased, trying to poke fun at myself for having admitted my feelings to her yesterday. I rested my chin down on my forearm and chewed away on my bottom lip.

Maret crawled up to me and her soft lips grazed my cheek. I turned my mouth toward hers, but kept still. I wasn't about to be shot down if she had no intention of kissing me back.

But she did. She kissed me, sliding her tongue over my lips and inside of my mouth. She loosened her bathrobe and lay down next to me, pulling me in next to her.

Tonight her satin underwear was off. She put my hand on her breasts and led it down her stomach until moving it around on a soft spot that seemed to make her breath heavier. She kissed me in trails and rubbed me until I was rock hard, then rolled onto her side, and then beneath me, as she guided me inside of her. She moved back and forth in a steady rhythm, the old metal bed squeaking beneath us. She let out soft, low moans. Everything seemed to be in slow motion. I planted my hands up near her shoulders and bent down to kiss her. She whispered in my ear, light whispers of how good I felt inside of her, and could I go a little faster, push a little harder. And I could. My mind blurred and all at once I felt weak and limp and my body jerked forward collapsing on top of hers.

She kissed me along my face, over my eyelids, and down to my chin. She cradled me, and pulled the covers up over us. I drifted off to sleep, but not before whispering, *I love you, Maret*, and hearing her soft voice murmur, *I love you, too*.

And the next morning as we all hugged Maret goodbye and she jumped in Mrs. Simone's car to be driven to Boston to board a bus bound for New York, I thought back to what Isabelle had once said about love taking different shapes and forms. I don't think Maret had told me she loved me because she felt a deep romantic love toward me. I think Maret loved me because I was her unexpected discovery that summer at the Sea Dog. She had loved me through all of her listening and guiding, and she'd taught me how to find my own way. And maybe, in some way, she hadn't expected that she would be part of someone else's healing that summer, especially someone like me who hadn't known how much healing he'd had to do, nor how much healing there was left to be done. Maret had told me one night during my first week that I seemed kind of broken. I had felt broken. I think she loved being the one to piece me back together again. I think she loved what she had found.

*****

The next week, Mother and I would be the ones to pack our bags in the car and be smothered with hugs and kisses from the folks at the Sea Dog. Mother would clutch Mrs. Simone, who I knew walked with Mother every morning on the beach, a sort of counseling session. It was clear how connected Mother was to Mrs. Simone, and to all the others sifting through their own troublesome grains of life at the Sea Dog.

As Mother wiped tears from her eyes, and rolled down the window to blow kisses, I honked the horn and drove down the sandy beach road that delivered us to the highway headed back toward Ithaca. I rolled down my window and stuck my head out for air. Cars raced by and I felt ripples of queasiness flood my stomach. It was too hard to go. Mother pushed her sunglasses on and pressed a closed fist to her mouth, trying to hold back her tears in front of me.

"Well, it was a nice vacation, don't you think, Jack?" she said, her voice quivering.

"It sure was, Mother. The best one I can remember," I said.

She waved her petal pink handkerchief around in the air. "I mean I know it would seem silly to other people, paying money to go somewhere and being expected to pitch in like that, make meals, serve dessert," she said.

"I loved it, Mother," I said. "Thank you for taking me."

"Did you, Jack?" she said, pulling down her sunglasses and looking at me with teary eyes.

"I did, Mother. It was real nice."

"Maybe, we'll head back next year. Make a sort of tradition out of it. I'm sure Thomas would like it too. Not so sure what your father would think of the set up, but you never know. People change."

I was shocked that she'd even mentioned Father. She hadn't mentioned him in the past three weeks. I'd been the one to make the weekly phone call home to see how he was doing, and to let him know that we were doing fine on the Cape.

People change, she'd said. To me, the person that had changed was her. In those three weeks, her posture had relaxed, her smile had widened, and her laughter had flown out from the pits of her belly and echoed in the air. It depressed me that she thought Father would change. I would have bet my life that a man like him was content with being an asshole forever. Father acted the way he did because he could. That was why.

He wasn't going to change. If he wanted to change he would have done so by now. I was frustrated that Mother didn't see the things that seemed so clear to me now.

*****

We pulled into the driveway after a helluva long trip. The only light on in the house was in the bathroom. We walked inside through the kitchen door and I called out for Father. Mother scurried in behind me, rushing over to get a glass of water from the sink.

"On the john!" he called back.

"We're home!" I said as I ran upstairs and tossed my luggage on the closet floor, then put Mother's bags down in her room. I hustled back down the stairs and darted for the kitchen where Mother was already pulling food from the refrigerator and preparing dinner. Father came out of the bathroom and strolled down the hall. He rubbed his hands together real fast, then dropped the folded newspaper onto the kitchen table.

"What's for dinner, Claire?" he said, pecking Mother on the cheek.

He slapped me on the back as he passed by me. "Great to see you, sport!" he said.

"Hi, Father," I said, pulling out a bottle of milk from the fridge and chugging it down, staring up at the ceiling with a dreadful knot in my stomach that told me nothing was ever going to change with him. He wasn't going to ask about our trip to the Sea Dog, our drive back to Ithaca, nothing.

"I'll be in the den, call me when the food's on, Claire. Snap, snap! You've got a hungry man on your hands!" he laughed.

"Do you need any help, Mother?" I said.

"No, thank you, Jack. Go on and relax and watch the television with your father. I'll call you when dinner is ready."

I walked down the hall to the den, plugging my nose as I passed by the bathroom, then turned and plunked myself down in front of the tube. Father had left the bathroom door open. His rotten stench floated into the hall, taunting the savory smells from Mother's kitchen.

"Hey, Claire?" Father yelled from the seat next to me on the couch.

"Yes, dear?" she said as the oven door slammed shut.

"Claire, I forgot to flush the toilet. Smell's gagging me out here. Why don't you go in there and give it a flush for me."

I heard Mother's feet shuffle down the hall, the jiggle of the toilet handle, the flushing water, and the clicking of the bathroom door as she shut it closed. The kitchen sink water ran hard. Pots and pans clanked about on the stovetop.

"She was in the middle of making dinner," I said, shifting my spot on the couch, and leaning against the armrest.

"What's the problem, sport?" he said, staring at the television screen.

"She was making your dinner and you asked her to go and flush your shit down the toilet," I said.

"Who do you think you are using that language toward me," he said, glaring at me out of the corner of his eye.

"You haven't said barely a word to her since she's come home. She's been gone for three weeks, and you asked her to flush the toilet for you?"

"She was already standing, sport."

"She was standing in the kitchen, Father, not in the bathroom. And she was making your dinner. Goddamit, you're a lazy man." I jumped to my feet to leave the room.

Father jumped up, too, plowing me back against the couch. His face glowed a deep red, and the rolls underneath his chin shook back and forth. He was fuming so bad I thought for sure he was going to have a heart attack. The veins in his forehead turned a plum purple and protruded from his skin.

"Don't you ever talk to me like that, do you understand me? Do you fucking understand me?" he said.

"What's wrong with you?" I said, scrambling out from underneath him.

I fell over the arm of the couch and slammed backward into the door. He reached out for the back of my shirt as I stood to rush out into the hallway.

"Jack? Harv?" Mother called, walking down the hall.

142

Father sunk his bear like hand into my shoulder, hitting a nerve that sent me crashing to the floor.

"Father!" I said, wondering if this was really happening, was I really being attacked by my own father.

"You little shit," he kept saying. "You little piece of shit." The next thing I felt was his fist barreling into my skull again and again and again.

I cowered, trying to cover my head, trapped between him and the door frame.

"JACK! HARV!" Mother pressed herself in between us. Father dropped to the floor, gritting his teeth and snarling as his eyes grew wider and more crazed. Mother seethed, *"STOP IT! JUST STOP IT, HARV!"*

I muffled back tears and wiped the slobbering drool off my face. I felt the warm trickle of blood dripping down the side of my eye. Its warmth was the only thing I drew any comfort from at that moment. Then my mind went white and my head flopped into Mother's lap.

I woke to find our family doctor standing over me and shining a flashlight into my eyes. Mother was still on her knees. Her hands were pressed together against her lips as if in prayer. Her face was light as snow, and her eyes were dark as coal. She rocked back and forth, clutching her arms around her tiny waist, her fingertips gripping her blood stained apron.

"How do you feel, son?" the doctor said.

"I'm fine. Just fine, thank you."

"Let's get him into bed, put an ice pack on his head. Don't let him leave the house for 48 hours, no sports of any kind. It's a concussion. No doubt about it," he said, tilting my head from side to side with his cold hand and sighing.

My words felt jumbled in my head. The only thing I knew was that I didn't want to be upstairs in my bed. I didn't want to be in the house with my father. For the first time in my life, I was afraid of what he might do. He seemed psychotic to me. I had seen the look in his eyes when he'd raised his arm back and kept smashing his fist into me.

143

They were blank, completely blank. There was nothing behind them, not a drop of life, not an ounce of soul. There was just nothing there.

I wonder what they see, those types of people like my father. When their eyes go blank like that, what do they see in front of them? Because I don't like to think that a father could really see his own son in front of him and still want to beat the shit out of him. If you ever look into a person's eyes like that, if you ever see that empty stare that I'm talking about, then you'll know what I mean. It's the stare of someone who has flirted with the devil, I think. It's the stare of a man whose soul has escaped him and gone wandering around in the pits of hell.

I drifted off to sleep that night staring across the room at a family photo Mother had mounted on our wall when Thomas and I were real little. A snapshot of the perfect family, upper-crust, educated, all with pearly white smiles. Snapshots lie, don't they? They're a hook for the viewer's imagination, always making things seem better than they actually might be. A perfect house, a perfect family, frozen in time, so one day we can all look back and remember how good things used to seem.

THE LONGEST YEAR

What can I say, senior year in high school was just about the most god awful thing I had ever been put through. For one thing, all the upper class kids, the ones I liked to hang out with, had already left for college, and the ones left in my class with were so damn jolly about their senior year that it made me want to puke.

I applied early decision to Harvard, and found my acceptance letter in the mailbox by the first week of November. I was pretty happy about it in the end. Maybe Mother had been on to something the afternoon of the interview. Maybe I was the type of guy meant for a place like Harvard. Of course, getting in early only served to make my senior year seem more boring and pointless. I skipped my classes often and biked home to watch the tube on the days when Mother had her photography class at the local art school. Speaking of Mother, she'd been taking quite a lot of photos. She still loved taking shots of houses, but more recently, she focused on landscapes. She said she was curious about what was beyond all of those different horizons.

Speaking of new horizons, a letter arrived from Isabelle Whitney announcing that her family was moving to California. It was the first time I'd heard from her since I got around to sending her my letter from the Sea Dog. She said she cried to think of how far away California was, and that maybe one day she'd go to college back east and we might see one another again. I felt real down in the dumps the night the letter arrived. Damn time just kept on passing, and now Isabelle was moving across the country. I had written her that maybe we could meet up somewhere over Christmas break, New York maybe, or Boston. But it didn't look like that would work out now that she was moving. I promised to keep writing her though; we were still best friends after all.

Izzy wasn't the only one to move on. No one had seen from Father in months. You'd think this would upset a guy, not to see his own father and all, but after our last encounter, there was a void in my heart for the old man. There was just nothing there but a hollow spot. I felt alright about it, truth be told. A short while later, Thomas called from a Cambridge pay phone and said he'd received a postcard from Father saying he was in Boca. Mother didn't know what Boca meant, and she didn't bother to ask Thomas. I'd overheard her on the phone the other night saying she was ready to leave Father, if only she knew where he was she'd serve him the papers. She said she'd have to sell the house and move into some apartment on the south side of town. I didn't want my mother in an apartment, especially an apartment on the south side. I wanted her to have her big kitchen, and her garden, and the basement downstairs that she'd turned into a dark room to process her film. I wondered if Father would ever show his face again.

The winter in Ithaca was about as cold as an Arctic blast. I felt guilty when I thought of leaving Mother to freeze it out alone while I was away at Harvard. But her face had lit up when she talked about me going to Harvard come September. She said she'd never been prouder of anything in her whole life, except the night that she'd brought me home from the hospital and looked in on Thomas asleep in his bed. She said that seeing her two sleeping boys that first night I'd come home had made her feel so fulfilled inside.

When spring came around, the season of all things new, Mother and I drove down to the Cape and celebrated Easter at the Sea Dog Inn. It felt like a family reunion. The Willmots were back, and the young couple, the Morgans, were there, too, with a special announcement that a baby was on the way. We all raised our glasses and Mrs. Simone cried for joy. The magic of the Sea Dog had worked, she said. This time I didn't find the conversation about them conceiving to be so embarrassing.

The only person absent was Maret, though I'd rummaged around near the phone in the kitchen and caught sight of her name and number written on an index card and tacked to the bulletin board. I thought about jotting it down in case I should ever be in New York, but then I changed my mind. Instead, I clung to the chance that she might resurface the next summer and that I might see her again.

But summer came and all I saw of Maret was a picture she'd sent in a letter to Mrs. Simone. Mrs. Simone read the letter aloud over breakfast one morning, and in it Maret announced that she was staying in New York for the summer that year. In the photo, she was hugging a golden retriever and sitting in front of some fountain at a place called Washington Square Park, or so it said on the back of the picture in her wild scroll. I imagined going there to that park someday, sitting at that fountain, and watching Maret walk under the archway in the background of the photo.

Mother and I had gladly returned to the Sea Dog, this time staying on for six weeks instead of three. Thomas said he'd come down for a weekend from Cambridge, but I had my doubts. From time to time, I wondered about the new stories being spun down in Hyannis Port at the Honeysuckle, but then figured that even with fresh characters each summer, the stories likely remained the same.

I spent most of my days at the Sea Dog lying upstairs in room B and working my way through Harvard's summer reading list. Room A was empty, but it didn't seem right for me to take it over. It seemed that there or not, the room somehow belonged only to Maret.

I rapped on the wall each night as I fell asleep, sometimes praying for a miracle, that I would hear a rap in return, that she had been there all along, lying on the black metal frame bed in her white bikini, reading her glossy magazines, scooting up and pulling the tattered NYU t-shirt over her head, sitting on the heels of her feet and waving for me to come in. But then I'd wake up alone in room B, tilt my head back and stare out the small square window with the cloudy glass, and wait on a shooting star until I fell back asleep.

Mother took more photos that summer and Mrs. Simone framed them and hung them around the Inn. Mother found new friendships and rekindled old. And she reclaimed her youthful spirit as she dashed in and out of the Sea Dog with her camera swinging around her neck.

I buddied up with the young Dr. Mendel, an Assistant Professor at Hobart and William Smith Colleges in Geneva, NY. He understood the cold weather of Central New York, a fact that bonded us together like glue. Colin Mendel was the guy whose heels I would have tripped over if he were my older brother, the type of guy that would make one hell of a father. He dripped with a self-confidence that made you feel real secure just from hanging around him.

Dr. Mendel and I took up daily jogs. He saw to it that I was up real early, which got me to sleep pretty early, too. I found I liked the routine. Come to find out he had lost his fiancé to some illness in the past year. The guy was devastated. He had come to the Sea Dog to clear his head before heading back to Geneva in the fall. I told him about what it was that had brought Mother and I to the Sea Dog last summer, how fond we'd become of the place, and how I'd counted down the days until we could come back again.

"Has the place changed much in a year?" Dr. Mendel said one morning.

"Most of it has stayed the same," I said.

"But you were hoping to see your girl?" he laughed, knowing what I had told him about Maret.

"Yeah, I was hoping that part would have stayed the same, too." I felt a jabbing pain in my heart. And I knew why. So I told him how I'd been thinking about Isabelle, too. What a summer we'd had and how hard it was to cut it short like I'd had to. And how I wondered, would I ever see these people again? These people who I just couldn't forget.

We kept jogging.

"People leave your life, you know," Professor Mendel said. "People who you'd just as soon keep real close to your side. Sometimes they tell you they're going, and sometimes they don't. And you wake up one day and find out that the only person you can count on staying by your side is yourself. So keep doing what you're doing, Jack."

"What am I doing?" I said, hanging onto his every word, believing that he had wisdom about my life that I hadn't yet uncovered.

"Finding yourself. Keep making the most of yourself, Jack. And stop every now and then to open the door and let someone into your life, even invite them to stay awhile," he said.

"I can do that," I said.

"Of course you can," he said, punching me in the arm as he picked up speed and raced me around the bend that brought us back to the Inn.

When Mother and I packed up the car that summer, and everyone hugged and kissed us goodbye, the young professor, whom I'd heard sobbing away in his room each night over the loss of his fiancé, grabbed me in a hug and told me to make him proud up there in Cambridge. And at that moment, I knew the very thing that I had found at the Sea Dog that year. I had found the strong character of a man that I wanted to be like when I got older. I discovered another part of me.

HARVARD

Father had written a postcard wishing me luck at Harvard. It was the first I'd heard from him since the holidays. It had arrived the day we were packing up the car for school. Lucky for me, it was just my stuff that needed packing as Thomas has gone back to Cambridge early for football. I packed everything I could think of, including the last letter I'd received from Izzy saying that her family was west coast bound.

"Mother?" I said, cramming my suitcase into the trunk.

"Yes, Jack," she said, giving it an extra nudge.

"I wrote a few letters to Isabelle Whitney. When she writes back, will you forward them to me at Harvard? I want to make sure I get them."

"I certainly will, Jack," she said, putting a small cooler with sandwiches in the front seat.

Mother had been insistent that she drive me to Harvard.

"You can take the train from Syracuse second semester," she said. "But this trip, this trip is one that I'd like to take you on," she said.

Mother snapped a picture of me with my clean-cut hair, standing outside my dorm. I hugged her goodbye and told her I loved her. She could barely speak, so she just kissed my cheeks, wiped her eyes, blew her nose, and waved her petal pink handkerchief at me as she walked backward across the lawn before turning and breaking into a small trot toward the street.

She was headed to the Sea Dog for one last weekend. I was glad she would have people there to go home to, if even for a few days. Going home to an empty house in Ithaca, drenched in sad memories, didn't seem like such a good idea.

After my first month on campus, I found Harvard to be different from what I had expected. It didn't live up to all those raucous stories that Thomas, nor Father and his friends, had boasted about night after night when talking about the good ol' days. Thank god for that. My world at Harvard put those stories to shame. I wasn't a part of their legacy. I had chosen to create my own.

HARVARD vs. YALE

Now, do you remember back to my day playing in the Honey Bowl? I know we'd all rather forget it, but wouldn't you know that was the first thought that crossed my mind as I pulled my Harvard sweater down over my head and set out with my buddies to go watch the Harvard-Yale homecoming game?

"Did your parents come up for the game?" Cheryl Stilton, my roommate Nick's sister, said as we pushed our way through the stands and found a place on the bleachers.

"Mother is coming down in the spring, Cheryl. Hard for anyone to catch much time with Thomas during football season," I said.

"What about your…," she began, when Nick nudged her quiet because he knew my family situation. Nick was the kind of guy you could tell your family stuff to. He was a real friend, Nick was.

Thomas played quite a game, and I was happy for him. Harvard beat Yale 16 to 4 and we hooted and hollered and headed out of the stands jumping up and down while everyone yelled out to this one or that about which bar they were headed to in Harvard Square.

From behind me I heard a voice that was hard to forget and turned my head real slow to catch sight of none other than Mr. Whitney. Wouldn't you know it, old Mr. Whitney at the Harvard homecoming game, all the way from California. I remembered back to the first time Isabelle and I had spoken. *Daddy wears Crimson, too*, she had said. He stood with wide-wale green corduroy pants, a brown tweed blazer, a dark wool felt hat, and a collegiate scarf hung loose around his neck.

"Excuse me, Cheryl, Nick, I see someone I know. I'll meet up with you at the bars," I said, brushing past them.

"Sure thing, Jack," Nick said.

But when I turned to find Mr. Whitney, he was gone. Shit, I thought. I shoved by a few people, saying my excuse mes and pardon mes, then stood up on my toes, and jumped up and down looking over the sea of heads.

151

"Mr. Whitney! Mr. Whitney!" I said, hoping he would hear his name and call back.

"Yes? Who is that calling me?" he said. So I called his name a handful more times and inched myself in the direction of his booming voice each time he answered.

I spun myself around and when I stopped I saw exactly where he stood. I rushed over and extended my hand. Man, was I beaming to have found the old guy. "Mr. Whitney! Jack Sullivan, sir. Honesyuckle Inn a few summers back?"

He cocked his hand and studied my face real hard like he was trying to remember an old war buddy or something.

"Jack Sullivan, sir. Of Ithaca? Remember the Sullivan family at the Honeysuckle Inn?" I smiled and nodded. Poor, senile old guy, I thought, waiting for his memory to kick in.

He turned and walked forward.

"Mr. Whitney?" I said, rushing to keep up with him. "Why, Mr. Whitney, I'm Jack Sullivan. I was friends with your daughter, with Isabelle. You were acquaintances with my father, Harv, both Harvard men. My brother, Thomas, plays on the team, had one hell of a game today. Sir?" And he kept on walking.

Rage filled me. I wanted to clobber the old man. That old son of a bitch knew exactly who I was. I know he did. Sure it had been a couple of summers, but it wasn't that long ago. I let a few folks walk in front of me and then followed behind him. He walked with a quick step, checking his watch, all the while looking around him. He raised his hand and waved ahead of him, then flashed his shit-eating grin at a blonde on the bench a few feet away. My heart dropped. It was her. It was Isabelle.

My stomach lurched and my skin went clammy like I was on the verge of breaking a fever. I stood shaking at the sight of her. I picked up my speed, stopping a few feet behind Mr. Whitney as he approached the bench.

"Ready for dinner, Isabelle?" he called out to her.

She put a thin paperback in her purse and looked up smiling, a smile that quivered and fell apart when she caught sight of my face behind him.

"Oh my god," she whispered, holding out her hand.

"Isabelle? Isabelle, what's the matter with you? Why you look like you've seen a ghost," Mr. Whitney said.

She stood up and swept past him, running toward me and clutching the collar of my sweater as she hugged me. "Jack Sullivan, is it really you?" she said.

"Ah, Izzy," I said, pressing her body against my chest. She rested her head on my shoulder like she had done each night at the Honeysuckle. She made her soft purring sounds, and then she wept.

"I've missed you so much, Jack," she said, shaking her head in disbelief, her eyes wet and teary.

"Ah, Jesus, Izzy. I've missed you, too," I said. "I wondered if we'd ever see one another again, Iz." I wiped a tear off her cheek with my knuckle.

Mr. Whitney huffed and puffed and stood back, never once making eye contact with me.

"You should have written me you were coming," I said.

"You should have written me to begin with," she said.

"I did write you, Isabelle. I did," I said. She looked at me with a furrowed brow, and I think she thought I was a liar, but I knew the only liar was her father standing behind her, raising his eye at me.

"Are you at Harvard, Isabelle?" I said.

"Heavens no, Jack," she said. "Secretary school."

"Are you here, Jack?! My goodness, you're here, aren't you? I thought you might be here to watch Thomas, but it makes sense that you're a Harvard man yourself.

"I wrote you, Isabelle. I wrote to tell you the news."

"I'm sorry Jack, but after we moved to California, I never received a single letter from you."

"And I wrote you again over the holidays. And your birthday, on your birthday, Isabelle, I sent you the picture of us from Provincetown."

"Isabelle, we have dinner reservations. Please say goodbye," Mr. Whitney said.

"I have to go, Jack," she said, her eyes dimming out like a fading stage light.

"Izzy, wait, let me give you my Harvard address, so we can write to one another again. There's so much to catch up on."

"Oh, Jack. I can't do that. I'm seeing a young man now," she said, twisting her fingers together as she spoke.

"Oh," I said, my voice flat as day old pop.

Mr. Whitney walked away, and Izzy looked after him.

"I really have to go now. I'm so glad that I saw you, Jack. It was like I was watching an old movie, and you just walked across the screen," she said with a smile so warm it could melt butter.

She tilted her head and bit down on her lip. "You really wrote me, Jack?" she said again, her devotion to her father the only thing standing between herself and the truth.

"I really did, Isabelle," I said.

"Oh, Jack," she said, bending her head forward, shaking it and sniffling. She clutched me again, and I pressed my hands firm against her back, taking in the biggest breath of air I could before telling her what I had come to know.

"It *was* love that I felt for you, Izzy," I whispered in her ear. "That night when I said I thought I loved you, but I wasn't sure because I had never been in love."

"I remember," she said, pulling back to look at me, her eyes misting over as she rested her hand on my cheek.

"I know now. And it was. I love you, Iz," I said, feeling hot tears burn my eyes.

"I love you, Jack," she said, crying against her hand. "But I'm sorry, I have to go."

"Please take my address," I said.

"I'm seeing someone, Jack. And I'm pregnant of all things. And I really do have to go," she said.

"Oh, Jesus, Isabelle. Do you love him?" I said.

"I don't know, Jack. I just don't know," she said, crossing her arms over her chest, and nibbling on her thumbnail.

I watched Mr. Whitney on the sidewalk now, shaking hands with a young man in a navy blue blazer and loads of curly blonde hair.

"Is that him, Isabelle?" I said.

"Yes, Jack. He goes to Yale. We decided to bring the families together this weekend for the big game," she said.

"Does your father know about the pregnancy?" I said.

"He does," she said, rubbing her arms. "Not too happy about it. Don't know what he's more upset with, my being pregnant or that I'm marrying a man from Yale and not *Harvard*!" She tried to laugh, but the sounds got caught in her throat and instead her face crumpled, and she whimpered and looked down at the ground.

"Isabelle, let's go!" Mr. Whitney called across the lawn, and the young man from Yale waved her forward.

She bit down hard on her lip, and then reached out for me. I pulled her back into the warmth of my body. I hugged her a long time, trying to make her feel safe and loved. I felt her whole body relax into mine. God, I missed how Izzy felt to me. My friend, my love, whatever shape she took, she was the first person I'd ever met who truly felt like home.

"I'm pregnant, Jack. And I have two men waiting on me," she said, shaking her head, wiping her tears, and pulling herself up straight and tall.

"I know, Isabelle. You have to go." I held onto her gaze because I sensed that this really would be the last time I would ever see her again.

"Yes, I do have to go. And as I was saying," she sniffled louder now. "I'm pregnant, with two men waiting on me, rushing me while I'm here talking to my dearest friend. Well, I'm a lady now, aren't I, Jack?"

"You are, Isabelle."

"And you're the truest gentleman of this bunch. So I'd like you to walk me across the lawn, please."

"Isabelle Whitney," I said, my sadness turning to joy, "it would be my greatest pleasure." And on we strolled.

155

"Hey, Jack," she said, her voice trailing off as she linked her arm through mine and rested her head on my shoulder while we made our way across the green.

"Yeah, Iz?"

"Do you think you'll ever go back to the Honeysuckle?" she laughed.

"Not without you," I laughed. "Though if you ever need a place to go, Isabelle. If you ever need to get away from the world for a while, I want you to remember the name of that place I went to on the Upper Cape. Can you do that for me, Isabelle?"

"Sure, Jack."

"It's called the Sea Dog Inn, up in Eastham. Mrs. Simone is the owner, and she'll always know where to find me."

"Thank you, Jack. I promise I'll remember."

And I prayed that she would. Isabelle was the type of girl that you just wanted to tuck into bed each night and make sure she slipped away into the sweetest dreams. It didn't seem like everyone felt the need to protect her in that way. She was kind of shuffled off into the fast lane from the get go.

When we reached the edge of the lawn, I walked over to Mr. Whitney and the Yalie.

"Jack Sullivan," I said, extending my hand to a stunned Mr. Whitney, and a goofy Thad Barker the Third.

"So long, Izzy," I said, and kissed her cheek.

"So long, Jack," she said, and kissed the tip of my nose, then gave it a final soft tweak.

We laughed and I could tell the other men were uncomfortable as they stuffed their hands deep into their pockets and stared away from us, waiting for our goodbye to end.

"Jack," she said, taking my hands in her. "It was just wonderful to see you."

"Likewise, Isabelle."

"I will miss you, Jack Sullivan," she said, smiling and pressing her forehead against mine, which made me smile and think of our old times. Eye to eye. Mouth to mouth.

"The Sea Dog Inn?" she whispered.

"Yes, up in Eastham," I whispered back.

"I'll remember."

*****

I walked around Harvard Square in a daze, going in and out of all the regular bars that Nick and I usually went to until I found he and Cheryl standing outside a pub with a bunch of the guys from our floor.

"Hey, Nick," I said, pinching his cigarette out of his hand.

"Hey, Jack. Glad you showed. Your brother came around looking for you. He said your father showed up at the game. They want you to meet them for dinner in the South End at a place called *Sbordones*. Six o'clock," he said, snatching the cigarette back.

"Thanks, Nick," I said.

I stayed out at the bars for a round, then hurried across town to catch up with Thomas and my old man. I hadn't seen Father since the night he went at me, the night he left Ithaca and never looked back. I was surprised by how fast my feet were moving to reach them. The faster I got there and got it over with, the faster I could return to Harvard Square and get in another round of beers with the gang.

I saw the red awning with white letters that read *Sbordones*. I ducked inside and out of the drizzling rain that had greeted me when I'd stepped off the T. Father was sitting by himself in a dim corner booth. Thomas must have been running late. Father stood up when he saw me and shook my hand.

"Where's Thomas?" I said.

"I had dinner with Thomas an hour ago. I wanted to talk to each one of you alone," he said, stopping to slurp red wine. "I thought if you knew Thomas would be here then you might be more apt to come."

157

"You were probably right," I said, sliding into the red leather booth.

"Harvard treating you well?" he said, slapping his hands together.

"Yeah, just fine. Listen, Father. I'm not real hungry, and you've already eaten, so I'm going to head back to the dorms now."

"I just wanted to say I'm sorry, sport. I'm very sorry." He began to choke up a little then. I felt bad for him as much as I told myself not to. He just looked so pathetic sitting there slumped over and fighting back tears. My pity didn't last long though because when the waitress set down another glass of red, Father winked at her and pretended like he was going to pinch her ass. Same old guy, I thought.

I leaned back against the booth, crossed my arms, and looked away from him.

"I came to tell you I'm moving to Florida for good," he said.

"Congratulations," I said.

"I called your Mother last week. I'm visiting Ithaca next weekend. We're meeting with lawyers, doing all of that divorce stuff. I'm sorry it had to come down to that, but I guess that's the way she wants it."

What bullshit, I thought. He was the one who had left, after all.

"You kids are too old for that custody stuff. I want you to know that my door is always open to you, Jack. I'm sorry for how I acted that last night I was home. You don't even know the stress I was under. Unbelievable what your Mother put me through. Anyway, I do love you. And I'd like to keep a relationship with you. So any vacations or holidays that you want to spend with me, you just go ahead and give me a call and we'll see what we can work out, alright?"

"Yes, Father," I said. Like that will ever happen, I thought, noticing he was leaving the ball in my court.

"And no reason to do the child support this late in the game. Your mother and I will pay your tuition with the money we get from the house," he said.

"Does Mother want to sell?" I sat up straight.

"Well, she doesn't have any other choice in the matter, sport. I mean she can't cough up half of Harvard's tuition by selling her fruity photos, can she?" He grunted and threw back the rest of the wine in his glass.

The thought of Mother driven out of her home in order for me to stay in school made me want to puke all over the table.

"She'll get her damn alimony, and I'm letting her keep everything in the house, all the dishes, even the furniture. That's a lot, you know, Jack. I don't have to do that either. I'm just being nice to her. She should have enough to pay the rent in an apartment, but she's going to have to learn to support herself. That woman's been living large off of my earnings for years. She'll see what it's like to have to make a real living for herself, and it's not easy, let me tell you, Jack. But this is the way she wants it," he said.

I gripped my fingers into my thighs. I was afraid if I let go of my hold I'd flip the damn table over onto him.

"And like I told Thomas, I don't want to worry about all that last will stuff. I'm not leaving you kids anything when I die. There's a lot of family money, as you know. You'll each get three hundred grand now, and that's it. Do with it what you want, but that's all you're going to get from me, ok?"

"Ok, Father," I said, feeling the need for a glass of water.

"Well then, Jack, the check will be deposited into your account next week. Call me if you ever need anything. And I love you, sport," he said, leaning over the table and giving my back a whack so hard I thought my teeth were going to fall out. Then he plunked back in the booth, sighed and wiped his forehead with his napkin.

"I love you, too, Father," I said.

He looked up at me, startled like. "Thank you, son," he said, dabbing his eyes with his thumbs. "Thank you." He choked up, then cleared his throat with a hard cough into his fist.

Because even though I hated him, despised him actually, at one time when I was a small toddler running around the house, I'm sure I did love my Father. I don't know if

I'd said it then, and I sure as hell was never going to say it again, so I was glad I'd said it to him right then and there. And it was clear to me that he was real glad too.

*****

The following Monday, I received a notice from my bank that there had been a deposit for three hundred thousand dollars into my checking account. God damn, I thought, shaking my head and staring at the slip of paper. The first thing I did was rent a car. The second thing I did was skip my 8 am class and drive down to the Cape, chain-smoking cigarettes, and stopping only for a coffee or a piss.

I followed the signs for Hyannis Port, trying to remember the road that led to the Honeysuckle. And I did remember. I drove real slow down the bumpy, sand road. I pulled down into the back lot next to the side door. I walked up to the screen porch, pulling the door back nice and long before letting it go. It hit the frame so loud it sounded like a thunderclap.

Maybelle Winson came running to the door. "Who's there?" she snapped, gripping a broom in her hand.

"Maybelle? It's me, ma'am. It's Jack Sullivan," I said. I was prepared to give the same speech to her that I'd given to ol' Whitney: Sullivans of Ithaca, guests at the Inn a few summers back, but there was no need.

"*Jack?* Jack! What in heaven's name are you doing here?" she said.

"I came to say hello, Maybelle. See how you've been doing. And to ask a favor."

"I am so happy you are here, Jack. Come on in and make yourself at home," she said. "My, oh, my. Jack Sullivan is back in *my* kitchen! Why you are a sight for sore eyes, Jack. What a summer that was, was it not? How's your Momma, my goodness, how are *you*?"

Maybelle and I sat on two wooden stools by the sink counter and caught up on the year and half since I'd last seen her over two ice cold glasses of lemonade and turkey sandwiches.. It was one of those wonderful reunions and I told her I looked forward to seeing more of her again real soon. She walked me out to the back porch and hugged me goodbye like I was her own son.

160

"I'm so glad to help, Jack. And so glad you asked me."

"Thank you, Maybelle. Thank you."

*****

My next stop was the Sea Dog Inn where I checked to see if Mother was still staying as a guest. I had never wanted to see her more.

"Jack, how nice to see you," Mrs. Simone said. "You've just missed her. She left last night after dinner to drive back home to Ithaca."

"Was she upset by my Father's call last week?" I said, looking away. "I figured she would have told you."

"She did tell me, Jack, but she was stronger about it than you might think. She's ready for it to happen. She knows it's time."

I stayed on and helped Mrs. Simone with the evening meal. I chopped up vegetables for the salad, then shook my head laughing as I thought back to the first time I'd helped with dinner when Mrs. Simone had rolled the red bell pepper at me and Maret had introduced me to the wooden cutting board.

While Mrs. Simone and I chatted about the latest guests, I poked my nose around near the kitchen phone, looking to see if any new messages from Maret might have surfaced. Mrs. Simone turned around and caught me red-handed searching that old index card with Maret's number on it.

"She was a special one, wasn't she?" she said.

"She was very good to me," I said.

"She had a way. She joined the Peace Corps, Jack. Amazing, don't you think? She'll be spending the next two years in Africa, rebuilding villages. Just incredible news."

It was incredible. And it was just like Maret to be out there helping rebuild someone else's world.

*****

The next month flew by with mid-terms and soon enough it was time for the trip home to Ithaca for Thanksgiving. Thomas has gotten himself a girlfriend, and they had flown down to visit Father's condo in Boca, so it was just going to be Mother and I.

Mother waited for me at the train station. She said she'd be honking her horn as soon as I hopped down from the train car. It was evening by the time I'd arrived. A quick sleet fell and car lights pointed at me, making it hard to see Mother in the crowd of people waiting in the lot, but I could hear the short blasts of a horn nearby.

I found her a few feet away. She was behind the open driver's side door, half her body leaning in to reach the horn, while her other arm reached high out in the open air waving her petal pink handkerchief. She began running toward me with her arms wide open once she'd caught sight of me. Her feet slipped along in the wet slush.

"Jack! Jack, you're a young man, now!" she said as if I had been gone for years.

"Ah, c'mon, Mother," I laughed, giving her a hug. "It's good to be home," I said.

She sniffled and smiled. We walked to the car and I opened the passenger door for her, then threw my bags in the back seat. When I sat in the driver's seat, I reached my hand underneath the seat to see if there were any stray smokes around. Mother laughed and fished around her purse, pulling out her long brown cigarettes, passing me one, and then pressing her palm against the cigarette lighter. I laughed too, then lit my cigarette. I drove home with a gnawing feeling in my stomach, because to be honest, with Father and Thomas gone, and the house being packed up to sell, I wasn't sure what I was driving home to.

"Trying to pare down," Mother said as I eyed the living room full of boxes labeled *garage sale*.

The kitchen table was set for Thanksgiving dinner. We ate our turkey with the fixings and then Mother told me all the news that I had already heard from Father. I told her how he'd showed up in Cambridge, and she said she was sorry he'd done that. She cried when she talked about selling the house, and I told her not to worry.

"Hard not to worry, Jack," she said, dabbing her eyes with her handkerchief.

"Have you been taking many photos?" I said, trying to change the subject to something that might make her feel happy.

"I have. Here, let me show you some of them," she said, going into the living room and bringing back a shoebox of new prints.

I looked through them, amazed by her talent. My mother took these, I thought. I felt real proud.

"I went up to Eastham looking for you after Father came," I said.

"You did?" she said, refilling our juice glasses with white wine.

I sipped and nodded. "Mrs. Simone gave me a large box you had left behind. It was full of your photos. I brought them back for you."

"Thank you, Jack," she said. "I don't know how I could have left those behind. Almost every photo I've ever taken is in that box. I'd brought them along on my last trip to the Sea Dog so I could share then with Mrs. Simone."

"Stay here, Mother. I'll be right back," I said, running upstairs and grabbing my duffel bag. I yanked it down to the kitchen, pulled it over to the table, sat down and searched under my wool sweaters and long underwear until I fished out a blue binder.

"Here, Mother, this is for you," I said. "Happy Thanksgiving."

She took the binder from my hands with the look of someone who hadn't been surprised with a gift in too long a time.

"A present for me? On Thanksgiving?" she said. "Oh, Jack. I'm overjoyed!"

I sipped my wine and sat back to watch as she flipped back the cover of the binder, turned the first page, and covered her mouth with her hand.

"My pictures!" she said. "Jack, my pictures! You've had them bound! How beautiful!"

"I went through the box and pulled out a bunch that I thought you'd like to have saved real nice. You know, so you could show people and stuff."

"Thank you, Jack. And these are all my house pictures, too. I love these pictures the most, but I think you know that," she said as if she were looking at them for the first time. Those photos must have stirred up a lot of memory for her because all of a sudden she began to cry.

"I remember how you told me that you had tried to imagine living in those houses, tried to imagine them as if they were your home," I said.

"Yes, that's what I did," she said, nodding with a soft smile.

She pulled her chair around closer to me, moved the plates to one side, and positioned the binder in the middle of the table. She pointed to each picture, giving me the background on when it was taken, what mood she'd been in that day, and a glimpse into her imagination as she thought up a story of what might be happening inside.

"What's this?" she said, coming to the last page, her index finger already pointed, prepared to share the next story.

"Do you recognize that house, Mother?" I said.

"Is that the Sea Dog? Why, yes! It's the Sea Dog Inn! Did you take this one, Jack?"

"I did, Mother. On our first trip out there. Not as professional looking as your photos, but I thought you'd like to add it to your house collection."

"I love it, Jack. Absolutely love it. It's a beautiful photo, and it belongs right here with the others. Thank you, Jack," she said, touching her fingers to her heart.

"We know what goes on in the rooms of that house," she said, smiling.

"Yes, that's one home you don't have to wonder about," I said.

She ran her fingers along the sides of the photo. My Mother loved the Sea Dog. I think she felt about the Sea Dog, the same way I'd felt when I was with Izzy. It was that first time in a long time when you felt a sense of home.

"Well, it's yours, Mother," I said.

"Thank you, Jack. I'll cherish this photo forever."

"Not the photo, Mother. The house. It's yours now, to live in."

"Jack?" she said, turning toward me real slow and staring at me like I was speaking another language. "I don't understand what you're saying."

"I spoke with Mrs. Simone when I went to visit. She said that she is getting too old to run the place. I asked her if she would ever sell it. She said she'd considered selling it more and more each year. I know that you have to sell this house, Mother. I know you have to find an apartment to live in. And I know that all your life, the one thing you've been hoping to find is a place that you can *really* call home. And so I bought it for you, Mother. I want you to have a house and a home that you love."

"Jack, where on earth would you get the money to buy that house?"

"Father left me a living will."

"That money is for you, Jack. For your *future*. I've had my turn. The time ahead belongs to you."

"Ah, Mother. I have enough money, believe me. And I plan to work real hard after I graduate. I want you to live where you feel happy. So are you happy?"

"I'm thrilled, Jack," she said through joyful tears.

"Mrs. Simone will help you run the place, until you decide whether you'd like to keep it as an Inn, or live there on your own, maybe have a boarder or two."

"Oh, an Inn! An Inn! I can't believe this; I'm going to have my very own Inn!" She jumped out of her seat, laughing and crying, and stomping her feet on the floor, then threw her arms around me and pulled me up and out of my chair, twirling and twirling me around the floor the way she'd done when I was a child. "Thank you, Jack! Thank you!"

I laughed along with her, sharing her happiness, until we both fell back into our chairs.

"Mrs. Simone would like to stay on there, too," I said.

"I wouldn't have it any other way," she said.

"And you would need a head cook, Mother, because Mrs. Simone said she wants to slow down a bit. And even though it's communal she won't be able to get out and do all of the grocery shopping, prepping, and organizing the meals," I said.

"Well then! I'll go out and find a cook! A real good one!" she said, giddy with delight.

"Well, I think I know someone who would be a perfect fit, Mother."

"Who is it, Jack?"

"Do you remember Maybelle Winson? From the Honeysuckle? I think she'd be perfect for the job. Old lady Gardenia never treated her right anyhow."

"Jack, if Ms. Winson wants the job, then it's hers!"

"Well, then, I'll let her know it's for certain."

Mother turned her sight to the photo of the Sea Dog once again.

"Oh, Jack. I'm so grateful for you. Happy Thanksgiving, my darling boy."

"And to you, Mother. And to you."

*****

That next summer snuck up on us and we were glad when it did. Mother was all moved in and settled at the Sea Dog. She and Father had closed on the Ithaca house last March. When we made our final drive from Ithaca to the Sea Dog there was not one person there to hug or kiss us goodbye. That was fine by me; it made it feel like there wasn't anyone that we were really leaving behind.

We gave the Sea Dog a small face lift. Thomas came down with some buddies and gave a fresh coat of paint to all the rooms. Thomas had graduated in May and wasn't too sure where he was headed in the fall, so all of a sudden the Sea Dog didn't seem like too terrible of a place.

Maybelle Winson nearly tackled me as she ran in to work on her first day. "Jack Sullivan! I always knew there was a reason you wandered into my kitchen that fine July morning at the Honeysuckle. I said to myself, Maybelle Winson, there's a fire in that boy's eyes burning wild for the world, and I knew you were going to turn out to be something real special. I just knew it!"

"Ah, thanks, Maybelle," I said as I took her hat and handbag, and gave her the tour of the place. Maybelle wanted to settle into the kitchen, so I said I'd catch up more with her later, but first there was something I needed to ask her. "Maybelle? About that favor I asked of you?"

"It's all taken care of, Jack. I'm glad you trusted me to do that. Happy, happy folks, let me tell you. Poor man nearly had a heart attack right there on the spot, and that sweet girl, why she just burst into tears."

"Thank you, Maybelle," I said as we gave one another a hug.

Then I headed toward the front door where I put on my running shoes and ran out toward the beach for a jog, visions of the Newspaper girl, Jenny Joslin, and her father, Mr. Joslin, delivering the Sunday papers in a brand new pick-up truck.

The winds were strong that summer. *Winds of change*, Maybelle said one night as she nibbled her strawberry shortcake on the porch with the rest of us during dessert. I gathered all of the dessert plates and brought them into the kitchen when everyone was done. I poured a cup of coffee, then hopped up onto the kitchen counter as Mother raced by me with an old 45.

"Hope this gets everyone dancing!" Mother said. She had hung tiny white lights across the wooden beams in the parlor. I smiled as the shadows of all the people dancing flickered along the walls. As I put my empty cup in the sink and ran the water, I noticed the bulletin board by the phone had been pretty well cleared. The old index card was long gone. I said goodnight to everyone, and went up to my bedroom on the second floor, leaving the attic rooms up for grabs for any young guest who might pass through the Sea Dog's doors. It felt nice, like I had graduated to the adult floor or something.

The kitchen phone rang as my body slipped into sleep.

"Yes, ma'am, I'll leave the message," a voice I couldn't make out said to the caller.

The next morning, as the balmy sea salt air slipped through my window and danced between the curtains, I rolled out of bed and threw on my running sneakers. I poked my head into the kitchen and said good morning to Maybelle who was making a batch of buttermilk pancakes.

"Message for you on the board," Maybelle said as she danced her way from sink to stove to wicker serving platter. "Must have been taken last night by one of the guests."

167

"Thanks, Maybelle. I leaned forward to see my name on a fresh index card hanging from a royal blue thumbtack stuck in the right hand corner. I didn't recognize the number, but I knew the name. Isabelle Whitney. The message read: *Young woman inquiring about a room at the Inn.* My heart flopped. I fumbled for the phone, dialed the number, and woke a groggy man.

"Is Isabelle there, please?" I said.

"Isabelle no longer lives at this residence," he said. It was Mr. Whitney, I knew it right away. "Damn early to be calling, don't you think?" he barked.

"My mistake, sir," I said, hanging up the phone. I scratched my head. Had he kicked her out? Had she left? I looked at the time, then laughed to remember that the west coast was hours before ours out east. Served him right to be woken up from his merry sleep, I thought.

Four days later, a call came in from the Boston bus station. The operator said a young woman would need to be picked up from the bus station in Woods Hole at half past 3.

"Mother," I said. "I have to take the car. Have to pick up some new guests."

I wasn't sure under what conditions Isabelle was coming to stay at the Sea Dog, or for how long, but what I did know as I sped along Route 6 to pick her up was that whenever, if ever, it came time for Isabelle to leave, she would leave having found herself a real home. And for the rest of my life, I would keep the door open to her.

ARRIVAL

I swerved the car into the station. Hell, I jumped out of it while the old thing was half-running. It wasn't hard to find her. She was sitting on a bench with her arms crossed tight over her waist and a small tan travel bag by her feet. She was looking side to side. I knelt down right in front of her.

"Isabelle?" I whispered.

She looked me in the eyes, a fierce look that simmered and settled when she was sure it was me.

"Jack," she hushed. "Oh, Jack."

She leaned forward and rested her body against my shoulders. I could tell by the way her body felt that she needed food and water. She seemed so weak, my Isabelle did.

It dawned on me then that there was supposed to be a baby with her. "Isabelle, your child?" I said.

She touched her fingertips to her lips, and shook her head. "Miscarriage, Jack. In the final month. Can you believe that? I can't believe that." She stood up real slow, like an old woman rising from a chair, then reached down sideways for her bag, before I picked it up, took her arm, and walked her to the car.

The wind whipped around that morning. Felt like it was swirling around bits of the ocean.

"There is nothing like a Cape morning to make you feel alive, is there, Jack?" Isabelle said.

I held the door open as she slid inside.

"Ain't nothing like it at all, Isabelle," I said.

We drove through fog and I swore the damn stuff slipped inside the car when I'd opened the doors or something because it felt real thick and heavy between Izzy and myself.

"Are you hungry, Isabelle?"

"Starving, Jack. I think I'm actually starving!"

She tried to laugh, but I feared she'd meant it.

"Maybelle Winson is the cook at the Sea Dog, Isabelle. You remember Maybelle, don't you? From the Honeysuckle?"

"Why, heavens, of course. It will be wonderful to see her again. Her food was the best part of that summer!"

She looked out the window, splattered with drizzling rain, and chewed on her thumbnail.

"No, that's not true. You were the best part of that summer, Jack."

I pulled the car off the road, and we just sat there for some time.

"You were the best part of that summer for me, too, Isabelle."

She bent her head down, and kept rubbing her hands together.

"I wrote you, Isabelle. I swear to God that I wrote you. You were the most important person in my life and I wasn't about to lose touch with you."

She shook her head and let out a half-laugh, half-cry. She turned back toward the window.

"I know, Jack. I know. Daddy admitted that he'd destroyed everything you'd sent a long time ago. I was sick over it for some time. I still am if truth be told."

She was crying now. "No one, and I mean *no one*, ever treated me with the kindness that you did. No one has ever spoke to me the way you did, made me laugh the way you did, made me feel *alive* the way you did. I wondered for some time what your letters said. Or that photo you mentioned sending, you know, the photo of us in Provincetown, I wonder what it looked like. I've had some dark days recently, Jack, and I've wept thinking about that lost photo, thinking of how nice it would have been to look at it during those rough times. How good it would have been to see your face. And how good it would have been to remember what happiness looked like on mine."

I slid over next to her and held her real tight. "I will always be here for you, Isabelle. I will always be right here." We sat for an hour or so. She cried and I listened and held her. I handed her my handkerchief, and she blew her nose loud as a car horn and we both laughed a little.

"Feel better, Isabelle?"

"I do, Jack. I really do."

We drove the rest of the way to the Sea Dog sharing our memories of that Honeysuckle summer. I pulled into the Sea Dog and Isabelle's eyes lit up like fireworks on the fourth.

"Welcome home, Iz."

"I'm so happy to be here, Jack."

JOURNEY

"How long is she here for, Jack?" Mother and Mrs. Simone asked in the kitchen after Isabelle had eaten a full meal and gone to lay down in my room for a nap.

"I'm not sure. No idea," I said. They both seemed to consider her just another guest with a reserved room, which bothered the hell out of me. "She's here for as long as she wants," I said.

"The small problem, Jack, is that there aren't any rooms available right now. The place is jam packed. And, well, I'm not sure how comfortable I am with Isabelle staying in your room. I know she is your good friend, I do, but I don't know that I'm ok with you two being *that* close," Mother whispered.

Mrs. Simone looked away and started rearranging the magnets on the refrigerator.

"She slept in my bedroom nearly every night at the Honeysuckle, Mother. Nearly every single night," I said as Mother's jaw dropped open and a magnet crashed to the floor.

"Well, then, I'll try to be fine with her staying with you now."

*****

I went out for a run. The questions surrounding Izzy's stay were tormenting me. I assumed she was here to stay for good. I knew I wanted her to, at least. And of course, she'd stay with me.

When I came back to my room, I tip-toed inside so as not to wake Izzy. She laid there with her hands clutching her stomach. She stared out the window.

"Hey, Iz," I said, sitting on the side of the bed closest to her. "How was your nap?"

"Wonderful, Jack. The breeze lulled me to sleep and wouldn't you know, but I had the sweetest dream."

"That's great, Iz. I'm just going to hop in the shower. You want to walk on the beach after?"

"Sure thing," she said, rising up and swinging her legs off the bed in a mechanical way.

"I'll just need to use the bathroom first. How nice that you have a bathroom connected to your room, Jack," she said as she went in, coming out moments later.

"I'll meet you on the porch swing in ten," I said, going in and blasting the shower water.

"See you there," she said.

On the toilet seat that Izzy had just used there were specs of bright red blood. It seemed such an odd sight, blood on the seat, and the blood of Isabelle, no less. I wiped it off with some tissue, then dunked my head underneath the showerhead and breathed a heavy sigh of relief. She'd come back to me. My Izzy had come back.

*****

I stopped to watch Izzy swinging on the porch swing before interrupting her. She looked like a young girl swinging like that. It made me smile.

"Ready for our walk?" I said.

"Jack! Yes, ready as ever," she said.

I walked her down to a stretch of beach that I had come to love, enveloped by the rocks and dunes, and set off the beaten path. We sank down into the sand.

"You want a smoke, Iz?" I said, fumbling with the soft pack.

"Oh, no, Jack. No cigarettes for me."

That kind of made me sad for a minute. Being on the beach with Izzy felt nice, like old times on the Hyannis Port beach, but different somehow. Izzy had always been my partner in crime, the one who I'd stolen smokes with when no one was looking. It made me feel kind of sad that she wasn't going to join me. I shrugged and struck my match. We can't preserve all the memories, I thought, lighting my smoke and shaking the flame out. But god help me if I wasn't going to try.

"The Sea Dog seems like a special place, Jack," she said, pulling her knees up to her chest and smiling. The wind blew real light through her hair. She looked calm and content. "So many kind people. Why, Mrs. Simone already invited me for a walk on the beach tomorrow morning. Isn't that wonderful? What a kind, kind woman."

"She's one in a million, that Mrs. Simone," I said.

"And Maybelle's cooking, why that hasn't changed one bit, now has it, Jack?"

I laughed. "Maybelle is the best cook on the Cape and Islands for sure."

Izzy started breathing real heavy, and interlacing her fingers again.

"Jack, I need to tell you something." All of a sudden, the features of Izzy's once relaxed face became tight. "I'm a bit worried about my finances, Jack. I traveled from California by train. Took me forever, but I just knew I had to get here. Now I have to figure out a way to stay. Rooms aren't for free, I imagine!"

"Isabelle, you're my guest. The Sea Dog won't accept a dime from you. Though I should tell you that there aren't any open rooms at that moment, but when one frees up, it's yours if you want the space. Until then you can stay in my room as long as you need or want."

"Thank you, Jack."

I leaned back on my elbows. She shifted her body toward me.

"So, *Harvard*. Do you know how happy I am that you are at Harvard, Jack?"

I smiled and felt the heat rise to my face. "You were always rooting for me to go to Harvard," I said.

"I used to have a secret dream that I would go to Harvard someday," she curled her chin down to her kneecaps and stared off at the sea. "Daddy always loved me, but he loved Harvard more. I think I only wanted to go there so he'd pay me more attention! But when it came down to it, I realized that Daddy hadn't dreamed of me going to one of the Ivys. No, if I had been a boy, he said, then he would invest the money. But he didn't see the point in sending a girl to a university when she'd only wind up staying at home and minding the children when all was said and done."

"How has your father been recently, Iz?"

"Livid! Why he is simply livid!"

"Did you leave home on your own will, Iz?"

"I sure did. I was still living at home through the pregnancy, and let me tell you that was no picnic. Thad and I had kept in touch by letters, saw one another over the holidays. We'd met when I was in New York at secretary school. I was living with my Aunt Nancy out in Stanford, commuting to the city. Thad's family lives in Stanford, too, right next door to my Aunt's home. Thad came home most weekends from Yale."

Isabelle pressed her lips together tight, narrowed her eyes, then shook her head. "Anyway, it all happened quite fast. But when Daddy found out about the pregnancy he cancelled the tuition check for school in New York, shipped me back home to live with him and Mother, and enrolled me in a secretary school out west. California was where I was expected to sit and wait until the baby arrived. Thad and I had planned our wedding for next spring, but my second thoughts on marrying him had turned final after losing the baby. Thad was just trying to do the right thing anyway. It wasn't what you would call a match made in heaven."

She pulled her skirt down snug over her knees, then rubbed her legs up and down.

"Are you cold, Isabelle?"

"Oh, no. I'm ok, Jack."

I rubbed my hand on her back and felt her muscles release. Soon she started talking again.

"After I'd lost the baby, well, I was just a mess. Real depressed over this past month, you see. I'd wake up in the morning and it's all I could do to get myself out of bed, take a bite of toast, or anything. Daddy had no patience for that. I thought, well, maybe if I go back east, be around my old friends, live with my Aunt Nancy, maybe then I'd feel better, more normal, you know?"

"How did your father take the news of you wanting to leave?"

"My father said that if I dared to move out of the house before I was properly wed, he wouldn't pay a dime for anything more for me in his entire life. And he said that my mother was in charge of looking for eligible suitors for me and I was not to meet any men on my own. Can you believe that, Jack? He wanted to sign me away to some handpicked Ivy League man so he wouldn't have to worry about me anymore."

175

"I can't believe it," I lied.

"So I stole three hundred dollars from his drawer and headed east. The only thing I remembered was the name of the Inn you told me about that afternoon at Harvard."

"You're so brave, Isabelle. And I'm real proud of you."

Isabelle got choked up. "See, Jack? That's what I meant earlier. No one has ever spoken to me the way you speak to me. I mean, heavens, when is the last time someone told me that they were proud of me? I can't even recall. Maybe a schoolteacher when I was real young. But never in recent years, never until now, never until you." She laid her head in my lap and wept. I stroked her hair, not knowing what to do or what to say. A lump formed in my throat, and when I looked down at my sweet, distraught Izzy, I sunk my teeth into my bottom lip as hard as I could; it was all I could to do to keep from weeping along with her.

*****

Izzy fell asleep in my bed on her first night's stay while I laid out a rollaway on the floor for myself. It was hard figuring out if things would be like old times and we'd just sleep in bed together. I wanted to respect her space after all that she'd been through. I can't say it wasn't a painful night, what with me lying down there on the ground praying that she'd invite me to join her in bed. But she didn't, so after listening to the clock tick by to the next hour, accompanied by Izzy's familiar soft purrs, I accepted my fate of sleeping on the floor for the night and fell asleep.

I woke to the door creaking shut and the wooden floor boards shifting in the hallway under Izzy's feet. I heard the slow pull of the front screen door, and remembered she was going for a walk with Mrs. Simone in the morning. I crawled up into bed, hoping to get in another hours sleep or two.

The sunlight blasted into the room, and I woke, looking over at the clock, not believing it was almost high noon. I heard sounds in the bathroom, and felt happy that Izzy had returned. The sounds at first were inaudible, but then I knew them well, they were the sounds of her tears, her sadness, all muffled sounding like she was trying not to wake me.

176

I pulled my old gray sweatpants on over my boxers and tapped on the door.

"Izzy, can I come in?" I said.

The cries came to a halt.

"Iz?" and I pushed open the door. "Isabelle?" She was collapsed over the toilet bowl.

"Please don't come in here, Jack. Please!"

Startled, I turned to leave, shoving my feet into my sneakers and darting toward the beach for a run. But it was too late, the memory of the blood soaked toilet and Isabelle's wails surrounded me.

When I came back from my run and went into my room, Isabelle was gone. I headed for the shower, opening the door to find a spotless bathroom. I turned around to find Isabelle strolling into the bedroom and putting a vase of tulips on the small bookshelf.

"Thought they might brighten the room a bit," she said, raising her shoulders real high and giving a quick shake of her head as they came down.

"They look nice, Iz. Hey Iz, want to take a drive later? Maybe go down to Provincetown for dinner or something?"

"Oh, sorry, Jack. I have plans with Mrs. Klock. Have you met her yet? Delightful woman. She's here on a holiday from her husband. Guess he gets her nerves all a jitter and she comes here each summer to smooth them out."

"Mrs. Klock, yeah, I know her. She's a great storyteller, Iz. She'll have you laughing all day."

"Oh, good!" Izzy said, traipsing out of the room.

In the shower, the water pounded my back. I felt a gnawing feeling that Isabelle was distancing herself from me. And I hated it. I hung around the Sea Dog during the afternoon, played cards with the Willmots, who were back a third summer, then took off for a drive to somewhere, anywhere, to get my mind off the fact that Izzy was so close to me now, yet felt further away than I'd ever imagined she could be.

177

*****

It was dark out when I pulled into the Sea Dog, but I could make out the soft lights on in my bedroom. I imagined Izzy tucked in bed, reading her books. I raced up the stairs to find her.

I opened the door and there she was, her head propped up by pillows, her eyes closed, and her book open and sliding out of her hand. I moved it away to the night table, covered her with a blanket, and turned off the light. I walked to the closet to pull out the rollaway, but then I heard her stir, and the sounds of her soft purrs.

"Jack?" she said.

"Hey, Iz. It's me," I whispered.

"Sleep in bed with me, Jack," she mumbled.

Part of me was afraid that she was sleep-talking. Ah, shit, I thought, not knowing what to do. What if I crawled into bed and when she woke in the morning she was put off that I was there?

"Izzy, are you awake?"

She giggled. "Half-awake. Come sleep in bed with me, Jack. Like old times."

I dropped my pants and yanked off my shirt and just about dove under the covers to be with her.

"I was beginning to think you'd never ask," I said as she pulled off her nightgown, and snuggled her bare breasts up against my side, then rested her cheek on my chest. I stroked her hair and sighed.

"I love you, Isabelle," I said, staring at the ceiling, feeling kind of vulnerable about everything.

"I love you, too, Jack. I love you most of all." Her purrs turned to soft, sweet snores and I fought back the well of tears that were brimming up inside of me. My chest grew tight and my breathing felt like it had stopped, so I grabbed the nearest pillow, pressed it against my mouth, and tried to stifle my sobs. Goddamit, I did love her. I really did.

I woke up to see Izzy pulling a breezy summer sundress on. I'd only wished I'd woken sooner so I could have felt her touch some more before she'd risen from bed.

"Plans with one of the guests?" I said.

"Oh, no, Jack."

"No?"

"Plans with you! Provincetown did you say? Because I think Provincetown would be a wonderful trip to take today."

I scrambled out of bed and leapt with joy. "Izzy!" I said, picking her up and twirling her around.

"Jack!" she said, throwing her head back and laughing.

"You're back!" I said, lowering her to the ground.

"I never left, Jack. It's always been me right here, even when it's seemed otherwise." Her feet softened to the floor. She pressed her forehead against mine, bit her lip, tweaked my nose, and smiled her glorious smile. "It's still me," she said, "it's still Izzy."

I hugged her, stroked her hair, then kissed the top of her head.

"Meet you down at the porch swing in ten?" I said.

"See you in ten," she said.

PROVINCETOWN

I reached out and poked her shoulder as I walked onto the porch.

"Ready?" I said.

"Let's go!" she said, hopping to her feet.

I opened the car door for her. "We'll hitch next time," I said.

"Is that a promise?" She smiled.

The car chugged down the sandy road. Izzy rolled down her window and propped her feet up on the dash. I cranked my window down, too, then fished out the pack of cigarettes from underneath the driver seat, taking one out and throwing the pack on the middle hump of the floor.

Izzy reached down and grabbed one for herself, then pushed in the lighter and laughed. "What's a trip to Provincetown without a smoke, right Jack?"

She was back; she really was.

I parked in an old church lot I'd come to figure was the safest place to park without getting ticketed. We walked down Main Street, repeating our last visit by stopping for clams at the same shack and eating them down on the beach, sitting in the same spot where we'd sat all those years ago.

"Jack, remember how we smoked marijuana last time we were here? Remember that?"

"Yeah, Iz. That was pretty wild. What a magical day, huh? Listening to that guitar player, walking the stretch of beach, and popping out of the dunes just in time for that old Portuguese woman to pass by us, pick us up, and drive us home. I can remember your singing in the backseat of her car, and resting your head on my shoulder. I don't know if I ever told you this, but I sure as hell was thinking it, you looked gorgeous that day, Iz. You were all freckly and tan and glowing and peaceful, you were so goddamn peaceful. I just couldn't believe it."

When we finished eating, Izzy led the way down to the beach. She pulled her ponytail down and her blonde hair just whipped around in a way that made me think of a horse's mane. She reached down for my hand and clasped it to her heart.

"How long can I stay here, Jack? How long can I stay?"

My heart pounded. "Isabelle, I'd be happy if you stayed here for the rest of your life. I'd be happy if you'd stay with *me* for the rest of your life."

She turned to face the water, her fingertips tracing her collarbone.

"I'll try, Jack. I'll really try."

I pulled her in to hug her and she was just tall enough that she could tuck her head underneath my chin. She and I were the perfect fit, we really were. She tipped her head up and lowered her eyelids real soft as if they'd been kissed by an angel. Then she looked up at me, her irises contracting as she studied what felt like every bit of my face. Her fingertips trailed from her collarbone to mine, brushing against the collar of my shirt as she reached her hand underneath the cotton fabric. Her fingers traveled up my neck, resting for a moment on my Adam's apple before grazing my lips, side to side. I couldn't take it any longer, so I lowered my mouth to hers.

Now I don't know if you've ever kissed a person who was hungry before. Hungry for life, hungry for love. But Isabelle and I must have been starving all of those years without one another because when we kissed each other I swore my whole body exploded. And when the pieces settled, it's safe to say, they settled as one, and inside everything felt completely full. Isabelle and I were whole. One body, one breath, one life. That kiss was more powerful than any ounce of lovemaking I'd ever known, not that I'd known too much, but you get what I'm saying. And I knew by that single kiss that Isabelle was the girl for me. A kiss is more revealing than any other intimate act, and don't let anyone tell you different.

We walked back to the car, arms slung around one another's waists.

"Hey Iz, one of Mother's cameras is in the backseat. Let's get someone to take our picture."

"Oh, Jack!" she said, then giggled as she pointed to a little nun shuffling out of the church door toward a station wagon.

I shrugged and smiled. "Excuse me, Sister?" I said. "Would you take our picture?"

The Sister beamed, arranging us by the car and talking about the perfect light shining down on us.

Izzy sat on the hood, and I leaned back against the bumper. She threw her arms over my shoulders, pressed her head up against mine, and I placed my hand on her knee. I couldn't see her smile, but I could feel it. My Izzy. My home.

*****

That night in bed, we giggled like school kids, but heck, we still kind of were, weren't we? Izzy pulled her dress off, but left her underwear on. I kept my boxer shorts on, too. I know we'd done that stuff once before, but things felt different now and I didn't think either of us was ready to rush into anything.

When I woke in the middle of the night, I found her sitting by the window and staring out at the stars. Her voice was real low and quiet and she was talking, I was sure of it. I thought I was dreaming, but it was real.

"Izzy? Are you ok?"

"Jack! You scared me," she said, wiping at her eyes.

"Who were you talking to?" I said.

She ran to the bathroom and slammed the door. I heard the toilet seat go up, heard the trickle of pee, the toilet paper roll, the sigh, that terrible sigh, and then the wails, the crash of the lid against the seat, and then the weight of Isabelle's body as it hit the floor.

I flung open the door and there she lay slumped over the toilet. Her underwear was soaked in blood, and there were streaks of red on the floor tiles.

"Izzy!' I said, falling down to the ground. "Do you need help? A doctor?"

"No, I don't need a doctor," she scoffed. I felt a poke at my heart. Izzy wasn't one to speak in a harsh tone.

182

"What's happening, Iz?" I said, trying to sound gentle, but afraid she'd hear my alarm.

"What's happening? What's happening, Jack? I'm losing my mind, that's what's happening. I'm losing my goddamn mind every time I sit down on the toilet, and that's all you need to know."

"That's not all I need to know, Iz. Why are you bleeding? Is it that monthly thing?"

"Oh for heaven's sake, Jack. How old are you? *That monthly thing?* No, Jack, I'm not menstruating, if that's what you mean."

"Well, how the hell am I supposed to know, Iz? I'm trying to find out what's going on so I can help you, and you're talking to me like I'm a fucking moron." I slammed my fist against the sink and she jumped, bumping her spine against the bathtub.

"I'm sorry for slamming my fist, Isabelle," I said. "I'm sorry for startling you."

I thought she might cry for a minute, but instead her eyes turned real dark, and trust me when I tell you that Isabelle's eyes were the lightest shade of blue that you'd ever seen. But now they'd turned a stormy sea green that almost looked pitch black and left me longing for the crystal blue waters that I'd come to know.

"Don't tell me you're turning into your father?" she sneered.

"Be careful, Isabelle. I know you're upset right now, but be careful."

"You're damn right I'm upset, Jack. I'm upset because I lost my child a few months ago and you haven't said a damn thing about it. What is *wrong* with you?"

I couldn't breathe. She was right.

"I'm sorry, Isabelle. I'm really sorry that happened to you. I don't know what else to say."

"I lost my child when she, it was a girl you know, when she was full-term, Jack. Do you have any idea what that means?"

I slouched down to the ground. "No," I said.

"It means that child of mine was ready to be born. Why all she needed was a heartbeat. But no, for some reason or other she died, and there I wound up in the hospital

183

having to deliver her, actually deliver her, my dead child. They had me pushing, pushing real hard, Jack. And while all the other mothers on the floor pushed out baby girls that cried, and who the nurses wrapped in precious pink blankets and nestled right in their arms, my baby didn't make a sound. No, my baby was put into a garbage bag right in front of my eyes, and thrown into the waste bin. Garbage, Jack. They threw her in the *garbage*. They didn't even ask me if I'd like to see her, hold her even. I didn't care that she wasn't breathing, what I cared about was my sweet baby girl. And I wanted to see her, Jack. I wanted to hold her. And now I'll never know. Never in a million years will I know what she looked like, or what she felt like in my arms. And my god, that's killing me, Jack. It's just killing me not to know."

"Oh, Jesus, Isabelle," I sobbed. "Oh, Jesus." I shook hard.

Isabelle rubbed at her puffy eyes, then at her raw nose. She wiped snot on the back of her hand, then down on the bath mat. She got a hold of her breath and spoke real slow.

"And that blood you're seeing in the toilet bowl is my body purging out the rest of her, because even after all their goddamn scraping of my insides afterward, they said there was still some left that would bleed out on its own, a lot of it actually. And so that blood that's filling the bowl is of me, and her, and I can't even go to the bathroom without the reminder that I've lost her. And every time I'm done going, I'm stuck staring at that bloody bowl and wondering how on earth I'm supposed to muster the strength to flush the toilet and watch my child get sucked down into the goddamn sewers."

Isabelle's head toppled over against my shoulders and she sobbed for what must have been an hour. "My mother told me that losing a baby happens to a lot of women, Jack. That I needed to look past it and move on with my life like a lady of resilience. But what she didn't understand, what nobody seems to understand, is that even if it had happened to all the other women in the world, it had never happened to me."

She sniffled and her voice grew real quiet. "I feel like a childless mother, Jack. Like when people see me, they don't even know the woman inside of me, the mother that

I became the moment I found out I was pregnant. That mother is still in me, Jack. That's still me. And nobody knows that or sees that. But that's all I see."

Her sadness turned heavy with anger. "I left California and came out here to the Sea Dog because when I'd ask Daddy over breakfast why they had just thrown her out like that, why we couldn't have kept her and given her a burial at the family plot, he'd leaned over across the table and slapped me straight across the face, and my mother just sat there chewing on the end of the celery stalk in her Bloody Mary, not even coming to my defense. I came here because I needed you, Jack. Because I *need* you. And I need a safe place to heal." She sobbed.

I held Isabelle, kissing her head, and rubbing her shoulders. But I didn't mutter a word. I knew she'd been disappointed that I hadn't said much before, and even knowing that, I couldn't think of a goddamn thing to say. I hated myself for that, for being so damn speechless at the times it mattered most. But then I remembered what she had said to me that night I'd broken down outside the Honeysuckle and had told her about finding my cheating father.

"Breathe, Izzy. Just breathe." And she looked up into my eyes, and kept wailing. "Just breathe," I said, nodding and kissing her face, her eyes, the tip of her nose, the corners of her lips. And she did. She breathed, at first sharp, hard breathes because she was fighting for any air she could find, and then soft, steady breathes in tune with mine.

We rocked together on the floor until we heard a gentle tap on the bathroom door.

"Who is it?" I said.

"Jack, it's me, Maybelle."

Isabelle nodded. I opened the door.

Maybelle stared at the floor, the toilet bowl, Izzy and me.

"I've brought some breakfast up for you both. For some reason I thought you might rather eat together up here today, instead of down at the main table. Would that be alright?"

"That would be just fine, Maybelle," I said.

"Thank you, Maybelle," Isabelle said.

185

"Miss Isabelle, may I have some time with you in here, while Jack clears his desk and pulls over some chairs for your meal?"

"Yes, ma'am," she said.

I did as Maybelle said, then moved the food off of her tray and onto my cleared desk. I sat waiting, picking at the fruit cocktail, but not daring to take a bite until Isabelle joined me.

She was crying in there again and Maybelle was saying, "There, there, child. What you need is a Momma right now, that's what you need. It's alright, child. Maybelle will take care of you."

Half-hour later, the bathroom door opened and Maybelle slipped out as the pelting of the shower sounded from the bathroom. Maybelle turned around before she exited the room. "You are a good boy, Jack Sullivan. A mighty good boy."

"Thank you, Maybelle."

The shower turned off and Isabelle emerged fresh faced and clean in her lime green terry robe.

"I'm famished!" she said, pulling her ponytail high up on her head. She sat down and popped a few grapes into her mouth, smiling at me with her eyes as she chewed. And just like that, she was Izzy again.

*****

We rolled out of bed come morning and scrambled for our bathing suits and towels. We snuck out the back door of the Sea Dog to avoid joining the others for breakfast, deciding on a morning at the beach instead. Izzy floated along on a tube for a while, reading her book. I went for a quick run, then dove into the water to cool off. She came off that tube soon enough, and before long we were swimming together, trying to body surf off the small waves.

A few of the Sea Dog couples wanted to have a fire on the beach that night and Izzy and I went down to join them. Mother walked around taking lots of photos. She sat with us on our blanket for a while.

"I'm so glad you're here, Isabelle," she said.

Isabelle smiled. "So am I," she said as she put her hand on top of mine in the sand.

I couldn't believe it was August already. That meant it was nearing time for me to go back to Harvard. Ah, but I didn't want to think about that now. And what I really didn't want to think about was what Izzy would decide to do once it was time for me to leave. I was sure Mother would offer her a bookkeeping job at the Sea Dog. Still I worried that it might get a little lonely on the Upper Cape in the off-season for a younger person like Isabelle. Maybe she'd think about coming to Cambridge with me? There was no rule saying I couldn't have visitors. Maybe she could stay with me in the dorms for a few weeks at a time. Who knew? Right then, all I knew was that sitting by the fire, with my hand warm underneath Izzy's, felt perfect.

That night, we walked back to the Sea Dog while the bonfire was still going. The place was nearly empty. We went straight on to our room.

"I want to make love to you, Isabelle," I said, once I'd shut the door behind us.

"I want you to make love to me, Jack," she said, taking down her ponytail, pulling her shirt over her head, sliding her skirt down to her ankles, and slipping out of her underwear.

I yanked my shirt off over my head and hopped out of my shorts. Isabelle leaned up to kiss me, trailing the inside of my boxer shorts with her index finger before tugging them down.

We stood facing each other. Just like three summers before, we'd spent all this time sleeping in the same bed, cuddling up naked against one another, without really taking a good look at the other one. But on that night, it was pretty hard not to see the other, what with the full moon shining through the window and casting a long light on the floor.

"Your body is beautiful, Isabelle," I said, thinking that I should have told her that when I had seen her by the window in my room at the Honeysuckle instead of keeping quiet like a big dope.

Isabelle lowered her head, pushed a strand of hair behind her ear, and smiled. My god, she was gorgeous.

The years since our first time together had seasoned us. Having sex with Izzy at the Sea Dog felt not like a shameful first time, nor a tutorial session; it felt like making love. Whatever that is to you, or whatever you might imagine it to be, at nineteen, it was something that made me say a quick prayer that I might feel it again, because goddamn, it was unbelievable.

*****

I dug my duffel bag out of the closet, whacking it free from dust before tossing it at the base of my dresser.

"What are you doing?" Isabelle yawned.

"Mother wants me to fill the bag up with clothes that I plan to take to school. She figures they'll need another wash before being packed up," I said, crawling back underneath the sheets.

Izzy turned her shoulder on me and rolled to the far side of the mattress.

"Everything okay, Iz?" I said.

"Fine," she said.

"Listen, I was going to go out for a quick run. I'll see you soon?" I said.

When I leaned across the bed to kiss her, she closed her eyes and pulled the sheet up high under her chin, acting as if she were drifting back to sleep. But I knew she wasn't.

I rolled off the bed and walked toward the door.

"Jack?" she said when I turned the doorknob. I turned around. I caught sight of her worried face, and I frowned. I hated the thought that my leaving for school would upset her. She sniffled. "Jack, what will I do when you're gone?"

I went back to the bed, sat down and stroked her hair. "I was wondering that myself, Isabelle. I figured you might stay on here and work for Mother. Or if you wanted to move to Cambridge, I could help you with that, too. Heck, you could even sneak in and live with me in the dorms until we found you a place of your own. I'm sure no one would mind. After all, next year I'll be able to live off campus myself.

She turned over onto her back, pressed her hands to her chest, and burned her stare into the ceiling. "I just don't know what to do," she said, furrowing her brow. "I just don't know."

"We still have a few weeks before you have to decide anything, Izzy," I said, shoving my feet into my running shoes.

"Well, never mind about that for now. Have a nice run, Jack."

BACK WHEN

When I returned from my run an hour later, there was Isabelle with her own luggage bag thrown across the bed. She was shoving it full of her clothes. She was wearing her nightgown. Her face was flushed and puffy, and her hair was disheveled.

"Izzy? What's going on?"

"Oh, just packing, Jack. Figured if you were starting, then I might as well start, too."

I sat down on the edge of the bed, staring at her as she threw more of her clothes in a haphazard mess. I unlaced my sneaker laces real slow and eyed her carefully.

"Isabelle, what are you packing for?"

She stood up straight and pushed back a fly-away hair. "Well, you aren't the only one with a place to be, Jack!"

"So where do you have to be, Isabelle? Where are you planning on going?"

She started crying and wiping her eyes with the backs of her fingers, her elbows pointed up real high with each wipe.

"I heard..." She gasped for breath. "I heard from Thad, Jack. Well, actually, I heard from my father. Apparently, when I bought my ticket at the train station in California, the ticket holder was real concerned about me, not looking in too good of shape and all. So she wrote down my last name and went calling all of the Whitneys listed in the telephone book, and before long she reached Daddy, who said that yes, he had a daughter named Isabelle. Well, silly me had told that woman where I was headed, the Sea Dog Inn being such a quaint name and all, and sure enough she told Daddy."

"When did this happen?" One of my sneakers fell out of my hand, landing with a thud on the wooden floor.

"This morning, Jack. Early morning. I went downstairs for a glass of milk and found the message on the board. The call must have come in late last night. I phoned Daddy and he told me the story. He then explained that Thad, my intended, was heartsick over my having left home, and, of course, over the loss of the baby. He told Daddy that he wanted to do right by me, and that he still wants to marry me."

The moment felt like I was watching a movie and I couldn't believe what I was seeing, couldn't believe what I was hearing.

"Isabelle," I said, slouching over and sliding down to the floor. "Isabelle, you are talking like you may be interested in his offer."

"Well, maybe I am," she said, shaking her head like she couldn't fathom my disbelief.

"But what about us, Iz?"

"What about us, Jack?" she said, still shaking her head.

"What about our history, Iz? I mean our days at the Honeysuckle, how close we were then, how close we've become now." I felt sick sitting there explaining all of this to her. Didn't she know?

"Oh, Jack," she said, waving her hand around in the air and gliding back to the dresser for more clothes. "That was back when, Jack." She plunked a few skirts on the bed.

"Back when what?" I said.

She put her hands on her hips and stared down at me, rolling her eyes and talking to me like I was some young kid pestering her on the school bus or something. "Back when, Jack. Back when we thought we were so old, but we weren't. We had only just started playing grown up, only just begun the dinner parties, the smoking, the drinking, the sneaking away into one another's beds."

"And didn't that mean something to you then, Iz?"

"Well, of course it did." Her hands crossed over her heart, her fingers reached upward and brushed along her collarbone. "Sure it did, Jack," she whispered.

"And doesn't it mean something to you now?"

She stared at me with eyes glazed over, just stood there staring, and then started shaking her head real fast with all of that tangled hair sticking out.

I rose up on my knees and crept toward her, grabbing her hands and pulling on them, hoping she would lower herself down to the floor with me.

"I love you, Iz."

She looked down at me. "I love you, too, Jack." And for a moment her voice drifted to some far off place. And I wondered where she was, and if I'd ever be able to find her there.

I stood up in front of her, half-laughing because it all seemed so insane and half-begging because the insanity was making me feel so goddamn helpless. "Then what are we trying to figure out here, Isabelle?"

"We are lovers of the soul, Jack, you and I. And that's the most beautiful kind, but it's not always the lasting kind."

I pulled away from her and sat down on the bed. I chewed the inside of my cheek and started shaking my own damn head. "Why did you come here, Isabelle?"

"Because you told me to. You told me that the Sea Dog would help me."

"And don't you want to stay longer?"

"No, Jack. Not anymore."

"Isabelle, I'm leaving for Harvard in a few weeks. But that doesn't mean I'm leaving *you*. We can make this work, Iz. Really we can."

"I'm sorry, Jack."

"So you're leaving?"

"Yes, I'm sorry, I'm leaving. And I am, Jack. I'm leaving. I called Daddy this morning when you were on your run. I'll be gone by next week. I have to return to school this fall. Only one year left and I'll have earned my certificate."

"Secretary school?"

"Sorry it's not Harvard, Jack."

"I didn't mean it like that, Isabelle. You know that."

"Well, anyway. The truth is that I am in a better place now. I can't stay at the Sea Dog my whole life. I have to finish school and find a job. Isn't this what you would want for me, Jack? In my own ways, I've healed. And lying in bed all morning, thinking about that phone call, well I realized that I'm ready to live again. I have a wedding planned, Jack. It's the right thing to do. It's not what I want to do, but it's what I have to do. I'm sorry if I misled you by coming here. I really am."

"Why do you have to marry him? You don't have to do this, Iz."

"But I do," she said, sitting on the edge of the bed and staring at her feet.

Why couldn't she see what seemed so goddamn right to me? Why didn't her heart ache for me the way mine ached for her?

"Isabelle!" I cried out in a panic. All of a sudden I felt real helpless. Things were spinning out of my control. "Come on, Iz. Run away with me." My eyes searched hers until she looked away toward the door. I flew down to the floor and faced her. "Remember Provincetown, Isabelle? Come on, what do you say, let's hitch that ride out to Provincetown."

"I'm sorry, Jack," she said. Her fingers rose back up to her collarbone and she skimmed it from side to side as little tears surfaced in her eyes and fell down her cheeks one drop at a time.

I walked to the door, needing to get the hell out of that suffocating room.

"Jack?" she cried out, breathless yet teary. She slid off the bed and onto the floor.

I turned and looked down at my beautiful, sweet Isabelle, a broken mess sitting in a heap.

"Ah, shit, Izzy. I can't do this. I can't lose you." I went over and sat next to her, tilting my head back against the bedpost, and pressing both hands against my forehead as I burst into a cry so painful it felt like all the muscles in my neck and face were tearing apart.

"Please let me help you, Isabelle. *Please.* I can help make everything better. You're telling me you've healed and you're better, but something in my gut is telling me that's not true, Isabelle. And I love you. I fucking love you. And that asshole from Yale couldn't love you like I love you, Iz. He just couldn't. He can't. Things aren't going to feel better if you escape into the life that you thought you had planned back then, Iz.

You're not going to finish school, marry this guy, and replace the real thing you lost that you want back the most."

"How could you say such a thing?" she cried.

"Because it's the truth, Isabelle. And I don't want you to be disappointed by your life. I know you would be happy with me. You know you would be happy with me. Please let me love you, Isabelle. *Please*. I'm fucking *begging* you. Let me love you!"

I bent over at the waist, holding my stomach and rocking back and forth. I cried so hard I thought I was going to puke. Izzy kneeled down and folded her body overtop of mine and held me.

"You already have loved me, Jack. You already have," she said in her soft, sweet purrs.

"But I'm not done," I sobbed. "I'm not done!" I collapsed to the floor. Isabelle collapsed down next to me, enveloping me with her body and bawling alongside me.

IMPRESSION

Isabelle didn't come back to the Sea Dog that night. I could go on telling you about the search and rescue squads, or the torn shawl that the police found washed up on the rocks, the same shawl she'd wrapped around her shoulders after dinner.

I could tell you about her walking out of the Sea Dog at dusk, but not before running back up to the porch swing to tweak my nose and kiss the tip. Or how she'd tilted her head and stared at me for a moment too long as if I were a stranger that she didn't recognize, only to slip into a misty eyed smile, her eyes a crystal blue, press her forehead to mine and whisper, "Love's been ours all along, hasn't it, Jack?"

I could go on about waking up in an icy sweat and feeling the empty spot in the bed next to me, the dent in the mattress, the mess of sheets. Ah shit, I could tell you about all of those things, but what good would it do me to drown myself in those memories and drag you down to the bottom with me?

"Remember this," Izzy had sung out as she kicked off her shoes into the overgrown grass and danced barefoot down the sandy path on her way to the beach. "You are my first love, Jack Sullivan. And my very best friend." Then Izzy had smiled that glorious smiled, turned away, and was gone.

Isabelle Whitney, she was my first love, too, and in many ways, she was my last. It was an affection charted over the course of summer months. A soulful crossing impressed upon the sands and lost to the ocean tides.

PRESERVATION

I walked down to the beach, lying down at the point where the water laps against the sand. I turned toward the water, reaching and grasping through each wave, but goddamn the water kept breaking. That's the thing about water-it's beautiful, but it never lets you get a good hold on it. Every time it comes to you, it just slips away.

"Jack Sullivan," a voice sang out from the dunes.

I turned around to see Maybelle sitting there, a plaid wool blanket wrapped over her shoulders, streaks of tears dried on her face.

"Hiya, Maybelle," I said.

"It's a beautiful world, Jack, but a troubled world. You touch the lives that you can, and you rest a bit easier knowing that you fought to make things better," she called out against the wind.

"I know," I said, my tears turning into anguished sobs for my sweet Isabelle.

"You're a good boy, Jack Sullivan."

"Thank you, Maybelle," I cried.

"You've done right by every person I've ever seen you know."

Maybelle caught her balance as she stood in the dunes, grasping her blanket, and walking down toward me. Her feet sank deep with each step. Her mustard yellow head scarf flapped in the wind.

She kneeled down next to my trembling body, then covered me with the worn blanket.

"I loved her, Maybelle," I bawled, clutching her hand against the blanket and rocking like a child.

"She knew that, Jack. And that girl loved you, too. That's why she came here. You showed her your love, Jack. Every day, you did. And she healed. Because of you, Miss Isabelle passed away at peace, Jack. She was troubled with her past, but her heart was at peace knowing that in a world that felt so lonely to her, there was one person who loved her the most, and that person was you. Miss Isabelle went to the other side, Jack.

And right now, I'm betting that she's up there in heaven holding her baby in her arms and looking down at you with a big smile. Can you feel it, Jack? Can you feel that warm smile of hers?"

I smiled through my tears. "Strangely, I can, Maybelle."

"And her heart is at peace, Jack."

There was nothing left in me to cry out, no matter how much I tried. I lay there limp and exhausted, lying in the wet sand while Maybelle sang a gospel song that I would never know the name of but would remember in my heart whenever a flash of Izzy went through my mind.

*****

On the fourth morning of staying in bed, only moving to pick food from the trays that Maybelle delivered, I heard a knock on my door. The clock on my desk read 6:00 a.m.

"Who's there?" I said.

A head of thick black curls poked into my room. I tried to make out the face in the dark morning shadows.

"Time for a run, Jack. Meet me downstairs," he said.

Holy hell, it was the Professor.

I wiped my eyes of sleep, threw on a sweatshirt, and shoved my feet into my running sneakers. I ran downstairs and found him stretching by his rusty sedan.

"How've you been, Jack?" he said.

"Been better," I said.

We ran for a half-hour before either of us spoke another word.

We were nearing the stretch of rocks where Isabelle's shawl had been found washed up, and my legs started to feel like spaghetti.

"I can't go any further," I said, turning around, gobs of saliva filling my mouth.

He turned around with me and we headed back. I picked up the pace, wanting to be off the beach. I ran straight up the creaky stairs of the Sea Dog, straight into the bathroom, and puked. Then I stumbled down the hall to my room, crashed onto my bed, and shivered and shook like some sort of addict going through detox.

The Professor came in and grabbed a clean shirt out of my dresser drawer. He told me to take off the wet one and threw the dry one at me in a ball.

The next morning I heard a knock on my door again. The clock read the same time as the morning before. I threw on my clothes and went downstairs. We ran for a bit longer this time, but in the other direction.

"How are you doing?" Professor Mendel said.

"Ok," I said.

The next morning I couldn't sleep, so I figured I would beat him to the chase. I got dressed, put on my running clothes, and went down to the room where he'd stayed last year. I checked my watch, 4:45 a.m. Ah, shit, I thought. He won't be up.

I tapped once on his door. He answered.

"Of course, I'm up," he said, as if reading my mind.

I waited for him downstairs. The air was chilly. I pulled my sleeves down into the palms of my hands.

"How are you doing?" I said when he pushed open the screen door and stepped onto the porch, chewing on the end of his sweatshirt drawstring.

"I'm doing," he said. "Feel like shit today, but I'm doing."

He picked up the pace and I tried to catch up with him.

"You?" he said.

"Feel like starting the world on fire, but other than that, I'm okay," I said.

"Ready for school?"

"One week and counting." I spit into the sand. "Probably will be good for me to go back."

"Classes good last year? Find anything that you might want to major in?"

"Nope, still floundering like a fish. Hoping it will hit me in my sleep sometime."

"So you're sleeping? That's a good thing."

"Yeah, I'm sleeping. It's actually all I can do."

"And running."

"Thanks to you."

"And the next thing you know you'll be driving to the store to get a quart of milk."

"Or a pack of smokes."

"Yep, those too."

"I'm kind of getting tired of sleeping."

"Why's that?"

"I just dream about Isabelle. It's making me feel like a fucking nutcase dreaming about her like that."

"Like what?"

"Like she's talking to me." I stopped and looked at him. "Does your fiancée ever talk to you like that?"

"Almost every night." He stopped and crouched down for a minute, taking a deep breath.

"Make you feel fucking crazy?"

"It did in the beginning," he said, popping back up and running again. "Now it just makes me feel good. You don't stop needing each other because one of you isn't there."

"Well, I fucking need her. I need Izzy." I stopped now, dropped into the sand, and buried my head into my hands.

"You know, there'll come a time when you might start feeling back to your old self, Jack, after the grieving has passed."

"Don't see that coming for a while."

"It'll be good though, when it does. You know that Isabelle is in a beautiful place, and you want her to enjoy that place, and not worry, right? You want her to know that the person she loved in you is still there and will be there for a long time. She knows you loved her more than anyone in the world ever did. She knows you miss her. And she'll be happy to know that you're going back to living your own life."

I stood and stretched out, then started running back toward the Sea Dog. The Professor didn't follow. It wasn't so much that I minded what Professor Mendel was saying, but that didn't mean I wanted to hear any more of it. There was truth to his words. I understood.

When I went back to my room after the run, I found Mother sitting on my bed. Mother and I had run our own courses that summer, both of us filling our days with the things we loved. For me, it had been Isabelle. For her, it had been teaching photography down at the community arts center. We'd catch up here and there over meals, and both felt a sense of contentment knowing how happy the other was.

Mother held a small photo album in her hand.

"Hi, Jack," she said.

"Hi, Mother," I said, slouching down next to her.

"My heart has been so sad for you, and for Isabelle."

"I know."

"I wish I was better with words at times like these." She ran her fingers alongside the album.

"I often wish that of myself, Mother."

"I put a little something together for you, Jack. Just a few photos I'd found of the two of you. They're from rolls on my camera. I developed them recently and had a nice smile seeing the two of you."

Provincetown, I thought. She was talking about Provincetown, the time I'd found Mother's camera in the backseat and asked the nun to snap a picture of Izzy and I. Izzy had wanted so badly to see that first Provincetown photo that her father had destroyed, and taking the second one was my way of recreating that for her. It made my heart break to think she would never see either one of them.

"Thank you for the gift, Mother."

"I love you, my darling boy," she said, kissing the top of my head before leaving the room.

I lay diagonally across the bed and stared down at the album, wondering if it was a good idea for me to open it and look now. I did. And I'm glad for that.

There were only five shots. The first one I had a good laugh over because I had never even known it was around. It was of Izzy on the sidelines at the Honey Bowl. Goddamn, she looked like a child with her soft round cheeks that had thinned in the past years. She was up on the balls of her feet, smiling and cheering. The next photo made my heart flip-flop. Mother was clever. Why it was taken of me and Izzy down at the tennis courts, our first real time spent together, a time when the very person I thought I wanted no part of became the opposite of everything that I had known to be true about the world around me. The third one was of me and Izzy this past summer down at the bonfire; that was the night we'd made love, real love. Would you know it, but the fourth was the photo of us that first summer at Provincetown, Mother must have made doubles. And the last was of us on our final trip to Provincetown.

I flipped back and forth between the two Provincetown photos and thought of all that had happened over those three years. I almost expected that Izzy would have looked changed in that last photo, that when I compared the two photos I would notice some look in her eye or something to tell me that she had changed. But the truth was that when I looked at her in that final photo, it seemed like nothing much had changed at all, not like in those moments when she'd fallen to pieces and broken down in my room. No, in that final photo, Izzy was beaming away like the girl I always remembered.

I closed the album and ran my finger along the square shape. It reminded me of the square window up in room B in the Sea Dog attic, the window I'd looked out of so many nights during my first and second summers, just waiting on a shooting star so I could make a wish and fall back asleep. I smiled to think that little would I have known then that one day my wish would be fulfilled, and at the Sea Dog no less. My sweet Izzy had come back to me. I took a final look at the last photo of us by the car in Provincetown and sighed for what I knew to be true, Isabelle Whitney had gone home.

GUIDED TOUR

I've been back to Harvard many times since I wore my cap and gown. The last time was when giving my daughter, Elizabeth, a tour. Goddamn, can't believe I'm old enough to have a daughter in college. She was bored by the place, which amused me. My wife, Anne, whom I met while working at a used bookstore on Newberry Street my Senior year, was laughing too.

"C'mon, Jack. She wants to go to RISD!" Anne said. "What are we doing here?"

"You really want to go to design school, sweetie?" I said, smiling at my little Elizabeth in her beatnik shirt and bell bottom pants, looking like she'd stepped out of my college yearbook, trying so hard to be unique.

"Dad, I *really* want to go to RISD," she said.

"Alright, RISD it is," I laughed, linking arms as she cheered and Anne gave her a high five. "Let's go out to eat and celebrate, how about it?" I said, but she didn't hear me. She'd already whipped her cell phone out of her pocket and was calling my mother at the Sea Dog to tell her the news.

We walked across the lawn and headed for the gate. Whenever I traveled that path, especially in the fall with the leaves crunching under my feet and that thick smoldering scent of autumn floating beneath my nose, it always made me feel eighteen again.

I looked over and caught sight of the bench, the bench where I'd seen my Izzy that afternoon of the Harvard-Yale football game. We'd looked at one another like apparitions, and today it just might be because I think I still see her sitting there. Her blonde hair pulled high in a ponytail, her plaid skirt touching the top her kneecaps, her paperback folded in her hand as she curls her chin to her chest.

When I grew nearer, I noticed that it was different girl, a real girl, who looked much like my sweet Isabelle. A young brunette rushed over to her and whispered something in her ear, and they broke into the endearing laughter of college girls. It made me smile. Before long, they were up and walking away. The bench was empty again. It almost made me want to cry seeing it so empty like that. I wanted to go over and sit down on it. I really did. I wanted to sit down on it so badly that it made my heart kind of hurt, really ache inside, just thinking about it.

Anne and Elizabeth had made it to the gates. Elizabeth's cell phone was still glued to her hand, but she was no longer talking, just punching away at the keys. What the hell did she call it, texting?

Anne looked at her watch and waved me forward. All of a sudden, I felt rushed, panicked even. Little beads of sweat spread across my forehead. I yanked on my tie to loosen it. I patted my face with my handkerchief.

My girls were laughing now. I faintly heard them, and clearly saw them. Anne grasped Elizabeth's shoulder with her head tilted forward. Elizabeth threw her head back, then wiped at her eyes. I felt like I'd gained a minute. Ah hell, they'll have to wait, I thought. I had my dearest friend to say so long to. What, with Elizabeth not going to Harvard in the fall, I didn't think I'd be back to Cambridge for some time now.

"I'll be right there!" I called over to Anne, but she didn't hear me. I hustled toward the bench, my steps clumsy as I raced to get there. I sat down, my stomach pressing against my belt. I'd packed on a few pounds since those college days. I rested my hand against the soft wood of the bench, chipped in places, worn and gray.

I closed my eyes and listened to the cheers coming from a group of boys playing football on the lawn. Run hard boys, I wanted to say. You'll be a middle-aged man looking like me in no time, gasping for air after making a lousy run toward a bench that holds some distant memory, a memory of a moment you were certain would turn into a lifetime. Goddamn time. Like I've told you all along, it just goes on and passes and doesn't check with you about any of it.

The breeze rolled toward me, helping me take in a breath and breathe, just like Isabelle would have told me to do. And the young man in me laughed time in the face. Then the wind rushed by me, a swirling wind that tousled my hair and tickled my nose and made me feel like taking up smoking again, if just for those few minutes. And then I heard her voice echo in the air.

Love's been ours all along, hasn't it, Jack?

It sure has, Iz. It sure has.

I heard a second voice, but this one was clearer.

"Daddy!" Elizabeth called out. "Daddy are you coming?"

I waved. "I'm coming," I said.

I stood up to leave, no sooner than a young man took my place, nodding at me as he passed, then pulling out a notepad from his weathered canvas bag as he sat down on the bench.

I waved over again at Anne and Elizabeth. "I'm coming, I'm coming," I said a little bit louder as Elizabeth ran over to me, laughing.

"Your old man's a bit slow these days, Liz."

"Oh, Daddy." And she wrapped her arms around my back and laughed while Anne beamed on from the sidewalk, love bursting from her eyes.

I looked back toward the bench, one final glance.

The young man wrote away like his pencil was on fire. A cigarette dangled from his mouth. All of a sudden, he stopped and stared off at the sky. Hell, he stared like he could see straight through it to the other side.

Ah, time. And on it goes.

The End